WILDCAT'S CLAIM TO FAME
JEFF CLINTON

A BERKLEY MEDALLION BOOK
PUBLISHED BY
BERKLEY PUBLISHING CORPORATION

Copyright © 1971 by Jack Bickham

All rights reserved

Published by arrangement with the author's agent

BERKLEY MEDALLION EDITION, APRIL, 1971

SBN 425-01983-7

*BERKLEY MEDALLION BOOKS are published by
Berkley Publishing Corporation
200 Madison Avenue
New York, N.Y .10016*

BERKLEY MEDALLION BOOKS ® TM 757,375

Printed in the United States of America

WILDCAT'S CLAIM TO FAME

Being the Story of How a Cowboy Named Wildcat O'Shea, a Lovable, Albeit Sometimes Rowdy Redhead, Became the Escort for a Noted Western Novelist During His Triumphant Tour of Redrock, Texas, in the Year of Our Lord 1879

ONE

Redrock, Texas, snoozed in the afternoon heat. The twisted main street, deeply shadowed at odd angles by the twin rows of clapboard, natural rock, and falling down adobe structures that lined it, was nearly deserted. The summer of 1879 had been brutal; not only had the weather been searing, but in July the town's leading madam had moved on to greener pastures in Kansas City, taking several of her best girls with her, and twice the weekly beer shipment had been late. The town needed a lift.

Struggling up Main Street, south to north, from the Big Dollar Saloon toward the office of United States Marshal Jack Jackson, came Wildcat O'Shea. Thoughts of the summer's dullness flitted around the edges of his mind, but eleven beers since noon had made his mental edges slightly fuzzy. More to the center of his consciousness were feelings of being somewhat hot, tired, bored, irritated, disgusted, and horny.

Now, to top all that off, Jack Jackson had sent a message that he wanted to have a conflab at once.

This could not mean anything good.

For Wildcat, it had been an extremely dull summer. But he was not so hard up for action that he welcomed a summons from Jack Jackson.

When Jack Jackson sent for you, Wildcat reflected dully, it always meant trouble.

Jackson was a lean, hard, fair, thoroughly honest, and competent lawman. Wildcat liked him. But through the years of their uneasy truce, Jackson had adopted the nasty habit of calling on Wildcat when especially difficult law-enforcement problems arose. Wildcat never helped voluntarily, because working with the law was against his principles. The trouble was, Jackson usually had some charge to hold over Wildcat's head, or Wildcat had broken something and needed the money, or something like that, and so Wildcat frequently had to help out.

Sometimes these deals were fun, once you got into

them. But it always went against Wildcat's grain. *He* couldn't help it, he thought with a vague sense of outrage, if he was the best marksman, tracker, horseman, roper, drinker, lover, fighter, and demolition expert in the country. After all, in most of these categories Jack Jackson was a close second, except of course the lover part, where nobody came close; so why didn't Jack do more of his own dirty work?

Nevertheless, when Jackson called, you went. That was the way it was.

Wildcat limped past the grainery and the post office, cut across the main intersection near the Hobnob House, and cut into the side street that led to the jail and Jackson's office. Wildcat was well over six feet tall and weighed about 225, all of it grit. He had fiery red hair, soaring ears, and a freckled countenance lighted by a grin that women usually found adorable despite the absence of two front teeth that had gotten in front of somebody's knuckles. Because he was between jobs and involved only in some casual drinking, he wore his everyday clothes: a faded blue shirt, green trousers, a red neckerchief and brown Stetson, boots that he had painted yellow, and his working spurs with the silver rowels. His only weapons were a single Colt, belted normally, and an enormous Bowie knife stuck in the thongs tying the holster.

For Wildcat this was, of course, conservative attire. Of the few people on the street, no one paid any attention to him.

Still maintaining a small piece of his pleasant beer buzz, Wildcat clomped up onto the porch of the jailhouse, opened the door, and stepped inside.

"Don't you ever knock?" Jack Jackson asked.

Wildcat slammed the door, making papers gush all over Jackson's messy desk. "Izzat enough noise for you?"

Jackson was a smallish, slender, stone-hard man with graying hair and eyes like granite. "You're drunk," he said disgustedly.

"You want me to leave and come back when I'm sober?" Wildcat asked hopefully.

"When would that be? About nineteen-hundred-and-six?"

Wildcat chuckled and straddled a chair facing the desk.

"I dunno. The way things have been going—"

"You make me want to puke," Jackson cut in bitterly.

"What did *I* do?" Wildcat expostulated.

"The way you waste your talent. The way you lay around and loaf. The way you get into trouble all the time."

"I ain't been in trouble for *days,* an' you know it!"

"Well," Jackson sighed, "it doesn't matter. You won't be getting into any trouble for the next little while, anyway." He paused and surveyed Wildcat with those stony eyes. "I've got a job for you."

"What other good deal have you got me? Impetigo? Trench mouth?"

"This is serious," Jackson said. "And important."

"Well, forget it, Jack, because I ain't going to do it."

"Well, I say you are."

"You got no charges hanging over me. I don't owe nobody anything, except my bar bill, an' that's normal. It's hot, I'm tired, I got a date with Rita in about an hour, my gut hurts, I think I'm getting flat feet, and my dadblamed toenails itch. I'm in no shape to do anything for you anyhow, and I *won't.*"

"This job," Jackson said, "you'll like."

"Haw!"

"You will."

"Tell me another 'n, Jack. When the chautauqua comes, you ought to get on the stage an' be this funny. You're a real riot. I think—"

"We're having a really important visitor come to town in a few days," Jackson cut in. "I want you to be the official escort."

"*Me?*" Wildcat was flabbergasted. "I'm the one you always try to *hide* from visitors!"

"This is different."

"He's got smallpox?"

"It's Ned Shipwright," Jackson said.

"*The* Ned Shipwright?"

"The writer. Yes."

"The guy," Wildcat said, suddenly beginning to get excited, "that writes the Western stories for *Cowboy* and *Thrilling Western Novels*?"

"The same," Jackson said disgustedly.

7

"My gawd! He's my *hero!*"

Still looking irritated, Jackson took a letter out of the desk. "He's coming to Redrock for a week or two. He arrives Saturday. He's on a tour. Looking for material."

"My gawd!" Wildcat cried. "He might write me up!"

"He says he's looking for local color," Jackson said. "The mayor and the town board figure you're it, if you'll behave yourself."

"Listen," Wildcat said enthusiastically, "I *will*, Jack! You tell me how I ought to act, an' I will! Grannies, the real Ned Shipwright. I got a bunch of his dime novels in my room right now. . . ." His voice trailed off, and he began remembering the vivid, exciting, colorful novels: *Flame of the Texas Rangers*, *Death to the Hombre*, *Bullets in My Chest*, *Texas Death Stampede*, all the others.

Lord, he thought, Ned Shipwright was a *real man*. He knew everything about the West, had been everywhere, had had all these adventures—

"All you'll have to do," Jackson was saying, "is stay sober and show the man the things he says he wants to see."

"I'll do it," Wildcat pledged.

"You'll do it?" The marshal was surprised.

"Jack," Wildcat said in a burst of candor, "I've patterned my life after Ned Shipwright."

Jackson frowned and studied his letter again. "All right. I suppose you could explain that. Don't—I don't even want to know. Now: the visit will be announced in Friday's paper. The mayor wants to talk to you right away. Go see him now. Incidentally, the job pays twenty dollars."

"An' all I gotta do is stay sober, an' show him around, an' talk with him, an' answer questions an' like that?"

"That's it."

Wildcat sprang up. "Boy, howdy! I'm on my way to see the mayor!"

The door slammed shut behind him, knocking all the papers off Jackson's desk again. Patiently Jackson began retrieving them.

The marshal's stomach hurt. It always did when he had to deal with Wildcat O'Shea. And the hell of it was that he basically liked Wildcat—even admired him. You had to admire him, in one way; behind the screwy exterior was a real mind, although the redhead seldom let anybody guess it.

Maybe, Jackson thought, the town board's gamble that Wildcat could put them on the map by impressing Ned Shipwright was logical. But Jackson had a premonition that he didn't like. Either Wildcat would do a marvelous job, or there would be hell to pay.

Jackson thought about what his friend had said about Shipwright being his hero, about "patterning his life" after the dime novelist's. *Was Shipwright another Wildcat type?*

"God!" Jackson said, leaning back in his chair.

"My boy," said Mayor Fred Watts, clamping pudgy hands on Wildcat's shoulders, "the future of Redrock may well depend upon you."

"I am gonna do it the way you an' Jack said," Wildcat replied solemnly. "I'll be sober as a judge, I'll be his escort an' bodyguard, what he wants to see I'll show him. Listen, he might not jus' put Redrock on the map, you know. He might put *me* in one of them stories!"

"Excellent, excellent!" The mayor beamed. "We'll meet Friday to discuss details of the welcoming celebration. If we wish to contact you in the meantime, I assume you will be in the vicinity."

"Well, I got to go out to Horner's tomorrow to do some dynamite work. Nobody else will do it; they say it's too dangerous on them cliffs, but I know how—"

"Excellent, excellent," the mayor agreed. "But be back Friday."

"You bet," Wildcat agreed.

"God bless you, my boy!"

It was the first time anybody in civic government had ever said anything nice to him, and it was invigorating as well as slightly disturbing. But when he left the City Hall Wildcat hurried back down Main Street, headed for Hilda's Place and his date with Rita. He was really anxious to tell her about it.

"You mean the *writer*?" Rita gasped, truly impressed. She had met him joyfully in her room, and stood now in his arms, her filmy black lace gown enhancing, rather than concealing, all her charms.

"Same feller," Wildcat grinned, hugging her.

"That's wonderful!" Rita cried, brushing a feline hand through her long, dark hair. "Why, that means I'll get to meet him, too!"

"I'm here to tell you," Wildcat chuckled. "Honey, you an' me are gonna be the biggest folks in Redrock the next coupla weeks."

She squeezed him. "Oh, darling, I'm so excited!"

She was, too. Wildcat, despite his own glee, noticed this in a variety of ways. He pulled her even closer, and began giving her even more to be excited about. Breathing heavily, she started to respond.

It was, Wildcat thought, just about the greatest thing that had ever happened to him. Meaning Ned Shipwright. But this, too. Hell, it was *all* pretty nice.

In the corner of a dingy saloon well off Redrock's main street, the two men huddled over their beers. They had taken care to be away from the other few customers, most of whom were in various stages of stupor anyway.

"Saturday?" said the one man, his evil little eyes blinking.

"That's when he gets here," the other man grunted. He, like his companion, was dressed in the dusty, nondescript clothing of a waddie, and had the same grimly desperate air about him.

"When do we do the job?" the first man asked.

"Frank and Burt come in Friday. We'll lay it all out then. But I figure we just stay close to him and watch our chance."

"Do you know what we get if we mess it up?"

"Do you know," the other man countered testily, "how much you and me are going to enjoy two thousand dollars apiece?"

"They catch us, they hang us."

"So we don't get caught."

"How about O'Shea? I heard O'Shea—"

"We can handle him."

"I don't want more killing."

"We'll do what we have to do!"

"I don't want more killing!"

"And I said we'll do what we have to do! Now do you agree with that, or do you want out of this deal right here and now?"

The smaller man licked his lips. "I agree," he said huskily.

"All right," the other man said grimly. "He gets here Saturday, and we move Saturday. And we don't let *anybody* stand in our way. Right?"

"Right," the smaller man said reluctantly.

"Good. Then there's no turning back now. We do it."

The smaller man almost spoke again. He was worried because he knew what a desperate adventure this was going to be. There was the odor of death about it; death for somebody else, or perhaps death for *him*, at the end of a hang rope.

But the stakes were too high to throw in the hand now. He said nothing.

TWO

The train bearing Ned Shipwright was due in Redrock at 3:08 P.M. Saturday, and the whole town was turned out by 3:00 just in case the train was on time. The side of the brick depot facing the platform had been festooned with the town's Christmas decorations. Across the track hung a banner on which the sign painter had emblazoned in purple, REDROCK WELCOMES NED SHIPRIGHT. There hadn't been time to fix the spelling. Townsfolk lined the platform. A box with steps had been rigged near the place where the passenger car would unload, so the visitor could say a few words. Here stood the mayor, members of the town board, and Miss Thelma Harper, the school librarian. The War Veterans' Club was off to one side. The Elks Lodge jug band and drummers' corps stood near the depot doorway, tuning up. It was hot and people kept craning their necks to peer up the tracks.

"Oh, where *is* he!" murmured Rita, turned prettily from the wind and struggling to keep her red velvet hat in place.

"It ain't even time yet," Wildcat grinned. "What time you got, Jack?"

Marshal Jackson, frowning, took out his gold pocketwatch, squinted at it, and replaced it in the pocket of his vest. "Five minutes yet."

"If it's on time," Wildcat added.

"If it isn't on time," Rita said, "we'll all be dirty and sweaty."

"I sure hope it rolls in soon, then," Wildcat said. He was wearing his best outfit: orange pants and vest with a new green shirt, light blue hat, yellow neckerchief, his good black boots with the big Mexican spurs on them (the ones with the rowels painted lavender), his gunbelt and gun, an extra strap around his middle to hold his knife in the flashy, handmade leather sheath, and a shellbelt draped over his left shoulder. He could smell himself; great waves of toilet water wafted up from his moist pores.

Over at the little speaker's stand the mayor had climbed

up and was trying to get people's attention.

"Our illustrious visitor will be here soon," he hollered. "We want a big, heart-warming, typical Redrock welcome."

A few people cheered. Wildcat good-naturedly surveyed the crowd, picking out familiar faces. His eyes slid over several men he didn't recognize.

"After the welcome," the mayor shrilled, "our illustrious visitor wants to observe Redrock in its natural state. So we won't have any parade downtown, or any big doings. We'll all just let him go about his business. This is the way he wants it."

Off in the distance, from the north, came the hoot of a train whistle.

"He's comin'!" somebody in the crowd yelled, and necks craned again.

The mayor excitedly climbed down off the stand.

"We're in luck," Jackson observed quietly.

Checking up on his shirt-tail, boot-shine, and so forth, Wildcat happened to glance again at the crowd. His eyes slipped back a second time to the strangers in the crowd. This time he caught himself looking hard.

Strangers were not uncommon, but these four men were well back in the throng and they didn't look happy and excited like everyone else. Also they were obviously together; friends. One was small, with little beady eyes and straggly black hair; another very big, bigger even than Wildcat, and black-bearded. The third was younger, pale-complexioned, with sky-blue eyes of the kind that Wildcat had learned to associate with violent men. The fourth, older than the other three, had a stubble beard, and a nasty scar tugged his facial muscles into a perpetual sneer.

Hardcases.

"Jack—?" Wildcat began, turning to call his friend's attention to them. But Jackson had slipped away and was on the far side of the platform, helping the volunteers keep the crowd from pushing so close to the tracks that somebody might get run over.

"Here it *comes*!" Rita said excitedly, hanging onto her hat.

The train had reached the outskirts of town. Its whistle blasted loudly, twice, and the crowd began to cheer. The veterans snapped to attention and got their flags standing straight up. The jug-band and drum corps struck up "Dixie," or possibly it was "Battle Hymn of the Republic." The dignitaries around the stand jockeyed for position, Ritz squeezed Wildcat's arm with excitement, men waved their hats, and here came the train. Then the engine rolled up to the platform, the smokestack hitting the welcome banner and tearing it to shreds so that it draped all over the engine and promptly caught fire, wheels skidding and smoking. The passenger car pulled alongside the platform, and then with a huge, farting noise the whole thing came to an abrupt halt.

The door of the passenger car snapped open. The jug band played louder, people yelled, the veterans saluted, the mayor stepped forward, down the tracks the engineer and the fireman tried to get the burning welcome banner off the engine, and in the doorway of the passenger car a shadow appeared.

Wildcat, despite his broad experience, was almost beside himself. He strained his vision for the first glimpse of his hero.

The first figure came into the doorway and stepped down. She was dainty, primly dressed in a dark traveling suit with a gray bonnet and veil, and she carried a small suitcase. She was cute, a blonde.

"Who is that?" Rita cried into Wildcat's ear.

Wildcat grinned. "I dunno, but I aim to find out."

Ordinarily Rita would have countered with a threat to claw his eyes out, but her attention was drawn back to the second figure coming off the train, a small, black-clad, flowered-vested, effeminate little man wearing a bowler hat on his head and a monocle glittering in his left eye. He had a gold-headed cane.

Wildcat gave this man only a glance, however, because at that moment the third person appeared in the doorway and stepped down: a huge, broad-shouldered, smashed-eared, hulking bruiser, wearing a rumpled pair of pants and bulgy sweater, with a big suitcase casually on his shoulder.

"That's him!" Wildcat said, nudging Rita. "Grannies, he looks just like I knew he would!"

The welcoming committee around the speaker's stand

had enveloped all three newcomers. The jug band continued to go berserk, although the applause had tapered off into a general hubbub and the veterans had gone back to Parade Rest. Within moments Mayor Watts climbed up on the stand and everybody, including the band, fell silent.

"Ladies and gentlemen of our fair city," the mayor cried, "this is a significant, yea, a historic day for all of us. We are being visited by a great American writer, a true lover of the West, a man whose daring exploits and dazzling pen have given all of us joy and pride in our gre-a-a-a-t American heritage." He turned and looked down at the newcomers. "We welcome you, Ned Shipwright. We are proud to have you with us. Thank you for coming, and may your visit be pleasant."

Everybody cheered.

The mayor beamed. "Will you say a few words to the people, Mister Shipwright?" He got down off the stand to make way for the novelist.

Wildcat found himself on tiptoes. His pulse hammered. The big bruiser moved. But only to get out of the way.

Wildcat stared, his breath hurting.

"Oh, *no*!" he whispered.

Ned Shipwright stepped up onto the stand, doffed his bowler to reveal a shiny bald head, and turned this way and that to acknowledge the cheers. The sunlight glittered on his monocle.

"No," Wildcat whispered again, wanting to weep.

"Friends," Ned Shipwright cried, in a voice that resembled a water pump with a leaky main valve, "I thank you for your welcome. I have seldom had one to equal it in enthusiasm or—" He glanced toward the band "—in volume."

He paused, evidently expecting laughter, and a few people dutifully chuckled. But it struck Wildcat wrong; he didn't like it, it had a—a *snotty* sound to it. Good cow, was *this* Ned Shipwright?

Shipwright, smiling thinly and revealing a gold tooth, was continuing. "I realize that a visit by a great American—and by Jove I am an American, despite my proud British ancestry—I realize that a great American seldom visits towns of this size or ah, shall we say, character. However, I wish to emphasize that from this moment forward I shall hope for privacy and, as it were, anonymity, in order to pursue my work."

He paused, took out his monocle, polished it, scowled, and replaced it. Hooking a thumb in his vest pocket, he continued, "I shall, of course, set aside an appropriate time for autographing my works, and for perhaps one lecture on the true character of heroism as I have lived it. Beyond these gratuities, I must reiterate my desire to work and be left alone. I know you will honor my wishes." He beamed, waved his handkerchief, and stepped down.

A few people applauded weakly.

"Why," Rita gasped to Wildcat, "I don't think I even *like* that man!"

The jug band was playing and snorting again, and Wildcat looked around to find an escape route. He was bitterly disappointed and mortified. His hero didn't just have feet of clay; why, Jesus, he was *clay all over*.

The welcoming committee, however, had split open, and the mayor was frantically motioning toward Wildcat.

"They want you," Rita said out of the side of her mouth.

"Not me," Wildcat grunted.

She dug her fingernails into his arm. *"Go."*

"Then, by gawd, you come with me."

"I have a headache," she announced, and turned and walked into the crowd.

His mind teeming with ripe obscenities, Wildcat went forward.

"Here we are," the mayor beamed, taking Wildcat's arm, the one with fresh fingernail marks on it. "Excellent, excellent. Mister Shipwright, may I present your escort, Wildcat O'Shea."

Up close, Ned Shipwright was worse. His eyes were about on the level of Wildcat's chest. If he weighed over 120 pounds, he was hiding it somewhere.

"Howdy," Wildcat said dutifully, however, thrusting out a hand.

Shipwright extended his own. "Well, thank you." He wiped his hand on his silk handkerchief very carefully.

"And this," the mayor rumbled, desperately jovial, "is Miss Millicent Stork, Mister Shipwright's secretary, and this is Mister Freddie Suggs, Mister Shipwright's valet."

Millicent Stork, up close, was startlingly beautiful in a cool, distant way. She gave Wildcat a slight nod and an ever-so-proper flick of her eyelashes. Cold, Wildcat thought admiringly. The thought of thawing her crossed his mind.

Meanwhile, Freddie Suggs, the gigantic man with smashed ears and nose, had reached out to mangle Wildcat's hand. Freddie's grin was genuine, and Wildcat was able to pour the power to his own handshake just in time to avoid things getting broken.

"Pleasure," Freddie grunted.

"Well, now," the mayor said toothily. "Shall we go to the carriage for the ride to our finest hotel?"

"Ripping," Ned Shipwright said sarcastically. "Freddie, see to the luggage. Millicent, a fresh cloth, if you please." He handed over his moist handkerchief, and Miss Stork produced a fresh, identical one from somewhere in the folds of her dress.

They walked across the platform to where the hack was drawn up. Actually, it was the mortician's hearse, but they had taken the glass sides off and aired it out, and put in new seats and some sideboards, and it didn't look half bad. There was even an awning over the top for shade.

Freddie began heaving the big suitcases and trunks onto the back. The crowd was breaking up, the band was dissolved, and the train hooted, preparatory to pulling out.

The mayor began to help Miss Harper, the librarian, up into the carriage.

"I say," Shipwright intervened, frowning. "What are you doing, there?"

"Getting everybody on board," Mayor Watts said, his face blank.

"Oh, rather, no," Shipwright stated.

"What?" the mayor said.

"We are fatigued from the journey, Mister Mayor. May I suggest that I, Miss Stork, Freddie, and this, ah, person in the abominable clothing take the carriage alone? I simply am not up to further conversation."

The mayor looked crestfallen, but agreed.

Freddie helped Shipwright climb up first, then jumped

up after him. Millicent Stork struggled up by herself, cooly ignoring Wildcat's offered hand. Cursing under his breath, Wildcat followed.

The driver clucked to the team and the wagon pulled away, turning, leaving the dismayed little group of welcomers behind.

The luck of the draw, and some slight plotting on Wildcat's part, had put him on one seat beside Millicent Stork, facing Shipwright and Freddie. Miss Stork showed no inclination to play kneesies. Shipwright immediately cast a disgusted look out at the main street as they turned onto it, removed his spectacle for more polishing, and scowled at Wildcat.

"I am very interested in you, sir," he said.

Wildcat felt a flutter of hope. Everything had been absolutely wrong so far.

"Well," Wildcat grinned, "I sure got a story to tell."

"By Jove," Shipwright shot back, "I hope not! I want an escort with color, not a conversationalist. You *are* the kind of man I ordered, are you not?"

Dumbfounded, Wildcat stared back. "What kind did you order?"

"The town ne'er-do-well," Shipwright replied matter-of-factly.

It got no better at the Hobnob House. It got worse instantly.

Several of the town's tougher customers were lounging around on the porch, chewing toothpicks, tobacco, etc., while awaiting a close-up look at the celebrity.

Shipwright jumped down nimbly from the wagon to the porch, and made a feather-dusting gesture at them with his gray gloves. "I say, stand back, there."

The nearest man, whose name was Jed LaRance, gave Shipwright a hard look. "You talkin' to me?"

"You and the others," Shipwright said frostily. "Stand back out of my way."

LaRance, whom Wildcat knew as a pretty tough type anyway, responded by swaggering a half-step closer. "People don't talk to me that way, Mister."

By this time Wildcat, Freddie, and Miss Stork were also down on the porch, and Wildcat had a chance to sort out names and faces. Besides Jed, there were Buster Davis, King Wilson, Dick Bruniston, Frank Street, and Jug Wonfor; a tough group, all troublemakers. Wildcat had had some fun with them a few times, but there was no love lost between him and any of them. They were the type that went around in a gang, looking for trouble.

As Wildcat recognized them, he knew that they would like nothing better than to spoil the town's nice little shindig by messing up Ned Shipwright's arrival at the Hobnob. Maybe they had planned it.

Even if they hadn't, the fight was about to start because Ned Shipwright, his face getting red with anger, stopped waving his gloves and slapped them sharply right across LaRance's chest. "I said step *back*, there!"

"Jed," Wildcat said quickly, "you guys jus'—"

He got no farther, because LaRance swung at Shipwright. The writer danced back quickly. "Freddie, deal with them!"

Freddie, who had been standing there like a statue, erupted into motion. He charged LaRance.

"Oh boy!" cried King Wilson delightedly, and they all charged.

Freddie hit LaRance flush on the mouth, but at the same time King Wilson hit Freddie, dropping him to his knees. The others rushed toward Shipwright, who looked like he was going to slap them with his gloves or say a nasty word.

Wildcat, disgusted, hit Dick Bruniston in the side of the head, knocking him against the wall and breaking a window. Miss Stork screamed. Wildcat caught a glimpse of Shipwright putting a protective, paternal arm around her—and getting both her and himself out of the line of action—just as Buster Davis hit in the middle of Wildcat's back, knocking him backwards into the street. The carriage team spooked and ran, dropping suitcases all over Wildcat and Davis, and just narrowly missing both of them with the carriage's back wheels.

Wildcat, irritated about getting his clothes dirty, brought his knee up sharply into Davis's groin, pitching him off. Wildcat sprang to his feet, getting up just in time to catch a haymaker on the jaw from either Bruniston or Frank Street, both of whom were on top of him simultaneously. Wildcat went down again, tasting blood. He was so disgusted with Shipwright that he couldn't even enjoy it. He bit somebody's ear and got a thumb in an eye. Street shouted with pain, and then Wildcat got a good left hand to Bruniston's face, knocking him backward.

On the porch, Freddie was just in the process of leveling LaRance with a roundhouse right that would have shattered a granite boulder. As LaRance went down, Freddie backhanded Jug Wonfor into the water trough and stormed down the steps to aid Wildcat. He slammed Bruniston in the chest, hurtling him halfway across the street. Wildcat, admiring Freddie's style, pounded fists to Buster Davis's face, chest, and areas well below the belt, bringing an elbow around as a finisher. Buster looked up with one eye and down with the other, and the one that looked down was looking in the direction he was falling.

Which was unfortunate for King Wilson, who was charging at the same time.

Wilson fell over Davis, and Wildcat got a good righthand shot at his face, a moving target, and brought up a blow from the ground. Wilson went stiff and collapsed on top of his friend.

Freddie was on his knees, bleeding, and Frank Street turned from him to come at Wildcat. Wildcat ducked his rush, tripped him, and went in to finish him off. Street rolled neatly and hit Wildcat on the nose, probably breaking it again. Wildcat fell sideways. Before he could get up, Freddie had staggered over and leveled Street for him.

All of a sudden it was very quiet except for interior heartbeats and the sniffling that both he and Freddie were making from leaky noses.

Wildcat gulped air and stuck out his hand to Freddie. "You're a good fighter, boy."

Freddie grinned. A tooth fell out of his mouth. "Yuh. You too, mate."

"Freddie," Ned Shipwright called impatiently. "If you are *quite* finished, see to the luggage."

Wildcat stared at him angrily.

"You," Shipwright snapped at Wildcat, "may help him." Then, before Wildcat could even swear at him, the author had turned, his arm still around the comely Miss Stork, to sweep into the lobby of the Hobnob House.

The Hobnob's finest room was big enough to accommodate a couple of beds, a desk, and several chairs. Wildcat and Freddie sat side by side on one of the beds, with Millicent Stork leaning over them, soothing their cuts and bruises with a cool, wet towel. Ned Shipwright, having removed his coat and vest to reveal a sweat-gray silk shirt, leaned back in the most comfortable chair, his feet on a hassock; he had unpacked a heavy, red leather notebook from the luggage, and was now soothing himself by reading aloud softly.

"The waterfowl, aghast against the sky, scans the ocean far," Shipwright murmured, looking down his nose through the reading spectacles he had substituted for his monocle. "Egad, if any o'er but I, had seen yon shimmering star. Twas fit for Homer or the Bard, I thought in murky gloom, this waterfowl a sky-black shard, the eloquence and elocution of doom."

"What in the hell," Wildcat muttered, "is he reading?"

Millicent Stork deftly mopped blood from his face, careful of his nose. "Poetry," she said, the tiniest glint of humor in her cool blue eyes.

"I never heard anything like that."

"It's unpublished," she sighed.

"How did Ned get it, then?"

"It's his. He wrote it."

Shipwright raised one hand and cried out louder, "Ah, this blinding fateful pain, the rack, the wheel of prosody's zeal!"

"*He* wrote *that*?" Wildcat said, glancing at Freddie for corroboration.

"Aye," Freddie grunted, applying a piece of tape to a cut on his jaw. "He writes a bloody lot of it."

"He has the soul of a poet," Millicent said.

"I thought he was a man of action," Wildcat protested.

"Be still, now," Millicent murmured, and made blinding blue sparks leap into his skull as she suddenly straightened his broken nose.

"You killed me!" Wildcat groaned through the tears.

She smiled. "Nonsense."

"She's fixed me nose a dozen times," Freddie said. "She's a practical doc, this one."

21

"I guess you've always got it busted fighting Ned Shipwright's fights for him?"

"*He* can't fight," Millicent said. "Not Nedwin. He might damage his writing hand."

"Ghastly groan of glimmering gain!" Shipwright exclaimed, holding the book high to catch the window light. "Silent, suffering, sibilant stealth! Be gone, beloved waterfowl, with might and main, be gone—be unaware of my withering woe in wealth."

Wildcat asked Freddie, "Does he jus' go around making folks mad, an' you bust 'em for him?"

Freddie grinned, making his split lip bleed. "Aye, but sometimes they make *me* bleed a bit, mate."

"Fighting," Millicent said, completing her work on Wildcat's face, "is a beastly profession."

"I don't make a business of it," Wildcat said. "Just a hobby."

Millicent eyed Freddie. "He did."

"You were a pro?" Wildcat asked with interest.

Freddie grinned again. "Eight-four bouts."

"Dreadful," Millicent shuddered.

"It's lucky for Ned that Freddie has that record," Wildcat pointed out.

Across the room, Shipwright snapped his book shut. "Freddie! Please place this back in the suitcase."

Freddie dutifully trotted over to get the book.

"All right," Millicent told Wildcat. "I believe you may go now, and wait outside."

Despite his disgust with the general situation, Wildcat had been taking in the way Millicent Stork was put together, and the way she moved it around. "Wanna meet me tonight?" he asked.

"You're awful," she said, but her voice didn't attain the frosty quality she might have wanted to pretend.

"I can meet you someplace," Wildcat said.

"Certainly not!"

Something told Wildcat that she didn't quite mean it. He was about to speak again when Shipwright beat him to it. "Millicent, please go at once to the local newspaper office and fetch copies of the editions about our visit. You may tell the editor I shan't see him today, but will grant a brief interview tomorrow."

Millicent jumped as if she had been touched with a hot poker. "Of course, sir."

"Freddie," Shipwright ordered, "accompany her. It appears that any decent person requires attendance in this beastly hamlet."

Wildcat got painfully to his feet.

"You," Shipwright said. "Stay."

"Me?" Wildcat said.

Millicent and Freddie went out. Wondering what was up *now*, Wildcat waited.

Ned Shipwright removed his reading glasses, tucked them in his shirt pocket, replaced his monocle, and rose to his feet. "You are well familiar with this hamlet and its environs?" he snapped.

"Uh, yep," Wildcat said.

Shipwright walked all the way around him, inspecting from all sides. "You do appear rather doltish, but you exhibited some grace in the momentary unpleasantness in the beastly street. I assume you know both the law-abiding and the unsavory elements in this place?"

"I know most people," Wildcat grated. He was getting angry.

"Bully," Shipwright said. "Tonight you will conduct me on a tour of the more colorful and interesting sections of the community."

"Like what?" Wildcat asked.

"The gambling halls," Shipwright said easily. "The houses of ill fame. The notorious bistros."

"I don't know if it's a good idea," Wildcat said.

"You were not asked."

"Yeah, but I—"

"Silence!" Shipwright screamed the command, and his face went crimson as he did so. He took a step forward, craned his neck back to look up into Wildcat's face, and started stabbing him in the belly with an index finger. "I—" he huffed. "AM—THE—FAMED—NOVELIST. MY—WORD—IS—LAW. Do you understand that?"

If it had been anyone else in the world, Wildcat would have flung him out the window right then and there. But he was stunned to inaction. This was Ned Shipwright. His *hero*, for God's sake! There *had to be* redeeming features in him; he couldn't *really* be such a squirt.

"I'll talk to Jack Jackson," Wildcat said, controlling himself with some effort.

"The opinions of your sheriff are of no concern. I have spoken."

"I'll talk to him," Wildcat grated, starting for the door.

"Stay here until Freddie returns," Shipwright said sharply.

"Why?" Wildcat demanded.

For the first time, Shipwright's imperious pose seemed to weaken. His shoulders slumped a bit and he glanced around nervously. "There is . . . good reason."

"You in trouble?" Wildcat asked quickly.

Shipwright caught himself slumping, and actually clicked his heels as he went ramrod straight again. "Nothing I can't handle."

"What, though?" Wildcat pressed.

"Threatening letters."

"Saying somebody is gonna do what?"

"Demanding money, or my life. Threatening to kidnap me for ransom."

"I better take 'em to Jack."

"I don't have them. I threw them away, of course. I give no credence to such tommyrot."

"Yeah," Wildcat muttered. "Only you want a bodyguard at all times."

"I'm not actually concerned. I only want to take no stupid risks."

"And you don't think going to the worst part of town at night a risk?"

"That," Shipwright replied icily, "is necessary to my calling as a man of American letters. To remain here alone now would be gratuitous disadvantage."

"But you figger," Wildcat said, "somebody might *really* try to kidnap you?"

"It would constitute a historic coup," Shipwright said. "But I doubt that anyone would dare."

"Because of me and Freddie, you mean."

"Because," Shipwright snapped, "I am more than a match for any shoddy band of desperadoes."

Wildcat groaned.

THREE

It was about ten o'clock when they started out on their tour. Wildcat, with a sizzling headache, a swollen nose, and the general discomfort of being stone-sober on a Saturday night, morosely led the way. Ned Shipwright wore a dark suit and a long, flowing black cape with a crimson lining. Millicent Stork, dutifully carrying notebooks and other writing materials, nevertheless looked serenely beautiful in her drab business outfit. Freddie brought up the rear, hulking.

Redrock had started to warm up to one of its usual Saturday nights. Horses lined the hitching rails in front of the saloons, and several men already snoozed in the black gutters between board sidewalks and dusty street. There was a nice little riot going in Herman's Café, and as Wildcat led his group past the place, a chair came flying through the window.

"By Jove!" Shipwright cried. "We should enter and observe!"

"You said you wanted to see the rough part," Wildcat growled.

"Well?"

"This is where the church people have their fun. C'mon."

They prowled deeper into the near-east side of town, the part where the real scroungy element hung out. It was not Wildcat's favorite part of town; strangers gravitated here, and drifters with bad trouble on their minds. But by God, Shipwright wanted the worst, and this was it.

Jack Jackson had been worried when Wildcat told him about the threatening notes and the rest of it. But the marshal had concluded glumly, "We can't keep Shipwright from doing what he wants. You'll just have to take him where he wants to go. And protect him."

"The way he runs his mouth, Jack, the Fourth Cavalry couldn't protect him!"

"That's your problem," Jackson replied helpfully.

Now, groping along the black alleyways, Wildcat led the way toward Billy Venters' Saloon. It was as bad as any of them, but Billy was a friend.

Several drunks staggered out of the blackness ahead of them and almost walked right over Wildcat before he could get them shoved out of the way.

"Excellent!" Ned Shipwright chortled, swaggering ahead and pointing with his gold-headed cane. "Consider the murky atmosphere, the black uncertainty and reek of degradation!"

As they had progressed deeper into the alleys, Millicent had moved closer and closer to Wildcat, and now he felt her hand groping for his. He caught it and clasped it. Her hand was ice-cold.

"I don't like it," she quaked.

"Hang on, hon," Wildcat whispered. "I'll take care of you."

They reached Billy Venters' place. It was an adobe hut stuck between a burned-out saloon and a black stone building that Wildcat knew was a place he couldn't explain to Millicent. Shipwright pushed open the front door of Billy's joint and led them in.

It was a big, square, earth-floored saloon with low, open-beamed ceilings flooded with the smoky light of lanterns hanging on wall pegs. Across the left and back sides the bar extended a glittering array of bottles and glasses on shelves. To the right were clustered tables, most of them occupied by men either drinking or playing poker. Toward the back was the wheel, turning through the haze of cigarette smoke. Doorways along the rear right wall led to smaller rooms where a man could have a private poker game, or just about anything else he wanted. The joint was fairly well packed.

Wildcat paused inside the door, still clasping Millicent's hand as he looked for a place to sit down. At a table nearby, two men sprawled on their outstretched arms, dead-drunk.

Shipwright, his cape flowing back dramatically, strode up to the table and shoved one of the drunks in the chest. He slid off his chair to the floor. Shipwright nudged the other one with identical results, and gestured at Wildcat, like a man summoning a waiter, as he sat down.

Wildcat took Millicent and Freddie over to join the writer.

"Splendid," Shipwright snapped, his monocle glittering as he turned this way and that to stare around. "Excellent atmosphere. Bully."

Wildcat sat down across from the writer, with Millicent on his left and Freddie on the other side. "You want a drink?" he asked hopefully.

"Of course!" Shipwright said. "Specialty of the house!"

Wildcat got up. "One jug of moonshine, comin' up."

Shouldering his way to the bar, he put in his order and turned to stare into the face of none other than Jed LaRance.

"Up and around, huh?" Jed growled.

"Just barely," Wildcat grinned.

LaRance scowled through a puffy eye toward the table where Wildcat's group waited. "I," said LaRance, "am going to break him up."

"I don't think you better try it, Jed," Wildcat advised.

"Not now," LaRance grunted. "I'm gonna be smarter. I'm gonna wait my chance *this* time."

"I don't think you better," Wildcat repeated.

LaRance turned and shouldered his way off into the mob.

Getting his bottle and glasses, Wildcat worked his way back to the table.

Millicent and Freddie sat there. Shipwright was gone.

"Where'd he go?" Wildcat gasped.

Freddie pointed, and Wildcat spotted Shipwright just strolling into one of the back rooms.

Wildcat put the bottle and glasses down, and hustled back there.

In the little back room, two men sat across from one another at a poker table. There was a chess board between them. One of the men was a farmer named Simons. The man playing him was a stranger, well-dressed, probably a drummer, about forty.

The drummer was hunched over the board, scowling. Ned Shipwright stood behind him.

"A suggestion?" Shipwright murmured to the drummer.

"No thanks," the drummer snapped.

Shipwright leaned over his shoulder and pointed to the

board with the tip of his cane. "Attack the castle. Queen's knight to bishop six."

The drummer said something obscene and instantly reached out to make an entirely different move, sliding his bishop along a long diagonal.

"Drinks are at the table," Wildcat said.

"Don't bother me," Shipwright snapped.

Simons, who had by now had a brief moment to survey the results of the drummer's angry move, reached out to make his own. He had a batch of his pieces all stacked up in the middle of his rear line, and Wildcat knew just enough about the game to realize that all those rooks and the queen and everything generated a hell of a lot of firepower up the middle.

Simons shoved one of the rooks all the way across the board and took the drummer's rooks in the back row. Then he looked up, his face holding that milky, expressionless quality that you usually see when a man is foreclosing your mortgage.

"Check," Simons said softly.

The drummer started visibly and leaned over to look at the unexpected crisis.

"You have to concede, of course," Shipwright announced.

"Shut up your damned mouth," the drummer said.

Shipwright pointed to the board with his cane. "You have accomplished a disaster. You must respond with knight to rook, and the other gentleman then counters with his second rook to knight, again check; you return your bishop to capture the second rook, he responds with bishop to pawn, check; your king must capture, he moves queen to bishop five, and checkmate."

Simons smiled thinly. "He's right."

The drummer stared hard at the board, then turned to look up at Shipwright. "Goddamn it to hell, what business is this of yours, anyway?"

"Your only hope," Shipwright smiled, "was a desperate Blomsbury attack along the diagonals. I tried to tell you."

The drummer, his ears fiery, began stacking the pieces up for another game.

Shipwright addressed Simons. "May I ask for a game, sir?"

"*We're* playing!" the drummer flared.

"You hardly offer competition," Shipwright smiled. "May I suggest you find a checkers player."

The drummer got to his feet, the chair going over. He was pretty big, and very mad. He was going to hit Shipwright, but as he turned, he saw Wildcat standing there.

Shipwright stepped back and motioned to Wildcat. "Deal with him."

The drummer, really angry now, spat a choice expletive and hurled himself through the doorway and out of the room.

"I wouldn't have done it," Wildcat said heatedly.

"Of course you would have," Shipwright smiled. "I should have maneuvered the situation so that you had to deal with him in order to protect your own life." He turned back to Simons. "Now, sir, about the possibility of an engagement?"

Simons reached into his bib overalls and took out a chaw of tobacco. "Don't mind if I do," he said. He was careful, but his pale eyes showed a hint of pleasure at the thought of what he was going to do with the slicker. Simons, Wildcat knew, was the county-fair champion.

Shipwright dramatically unfurled his cloak, tossed it over a vacant chair, and sat down. "You may use white. I must warn you that I have engaged in international competitions with excellent results."

"Set 'em up," Simons grunted.

"How," Wildcat interrupted, "about our drinks? I thought you wanted to look around."

"There is sufficient time. Return to the table. I shall summon you shortly. It isn't often one finds an opportunity to play chess in this wilderness."

Well, there was no use arguing. Ned Shipwright was a lot of things, and among them he was the stubbornest, hardheadedest, most cantankerous so-and-so Wildcat had *ever* met. He high-tailed it back to the table outside.

Freddie and Millicent had poured drinks. By the level of the bottle and the way Freddie's eyes were watering, he had had three or four already. Millicent sat cool and cleareyed, her glass untouched.

Wildcat sat down next to her and bumped his knee against hers. "Well, he's okay. Let's have some fun."

Her leg moved away. "It was such a long trip and I'm so tired," she said listlessly.

Wildcat poured himself a drink. "Drink up," he urged.

She raised her glass. Wildcat expected her to sip and make a face. But, obviously distracted and not thinking, she simply tipped the glass and drank it off. Neat.

No shudder. No tearing.

There was more here than might meet the eye.

Wildcat filled the glasses again. He managed to bump her leg again. *Bump.* She moved away again. Oh, well. "I guess you folks have it tough, traveling with this character."

"Aye," Freddie murmured, filling his own glass again. "But the pay is good, mate, and he does travel."

"He's a great man in American letters," Millicent murmured.

"Drink up," Wildcat suggested.

She did, neat again, deftly.

"You a school marm before you go to work for him?" Wildcat asked.

"No," Millicent murmured, still looking sad. "I was in entertainment. The legitimate stage."

Wildcat filled the glasses. "What did you do?"

"I was an actress."

"By gosh I'll say you're awful dadburned beautiful, if that's a help on the stage, an' I bet it is."

Millicent emptied her glass again. "Mister O'Shea, I have left the stage and the active practice of the arts in order to devote my life to the service of this great and much misunderstood artist whom we have accompanied here tonight. Personal happiness can only be found in such devoted and selfless endeavor."

Wildcat refilled again. He was beginning to feel a pleasant glow. "Izzat so?"

Freddie grunted, "He pays good. When he's writin', you ged a lod of time off. Only he ain't been wridin' mush ladely."

"He will again," Millicent said. "This trip will refresh his wellsprings. He is a great and beautiful man with the soul of a poet."

"Yeah," Wildcat said, fishing around with his knee and

encountering nothing but empty spaces under the table. "A gal as beautiful and sweet and—and everything—as you, she ought to be married."

Millicent drank again. *Gawd, if you just looked, you'd think it was water, the way she was pouring it down.*

"My life is one of selfless devotion and self-denial," she said.

"Only," Freddie rumbled, "he sure needs to be wridin', 'cause I thing he's runnin' outta money an' he ain't wrid anythin' for months."

"What," Wildcat asked Millicent, "did you play on the stage?"

"Life," she said. Suddenly her composure came apart and she giggled for an instant. "What else, stupid?"

"I seen her once," Freddie grunted. "Boy, boy." His eyes widened.

Millicent regained rigid control of her features. "Freddie!"

They had another drink. Wildcat began to get a buzz. The room seemed louder and smokier and hotter, and Millicent a lot closer and cuter. He wondered how the chess game was going. He didn't worry about it more than four-fifths of a second.

"I sure," he told Millicent, "wanna know about that stage career."

She giggled again. "You're a naughty man and you're trying to get me drunk."

"Aw! Why would I wanna do anything like *that*?"

Bump! Only it wasn't *his* knee which did the moving. "You are a *very* naughty man. Do you have to know *everything* about me?"

Feverishly Wildcat refilled the glasses. "Well, since we're all good friends, you know—"

"What is this we're drinking?" she asked suddenly. "My God, I feel all on fire!"

"Aw, it's just some fizz-water."

Bump! "Yes," she said throatily. "And it's starting to make me fizz."

Her hair had all fallen down by now so that it softly, sensuously framed her face. Her posture had gone slack and shockingly seductive. A button had come undone along her neckline. She leaned toward Wildcat, bumping him with several things she hadn't bumped him with previously.

"You're very naughty," she slurred. "You know my past and all about me, I bet. You think that just because I used to take my clothes off on the stage, I'll take my clothes off for you. Well, you're wrong. Wrong, wrong, wrong. I don't do that anymore. And you think just because you're so nice and big and tall and strong and handsome and funny and everything, I'll take my clothes off. You probably think I even *want* to." She drank her drink. "Wrong. Wrong, wrong."

"Aw," Wildcat grinned, "listen, honey, I got nothing but the very best intentions."

She nestled against him, her breath hot against his throat. "Oh, darling, I'm really soused. Please take me somewhere right this instant."

"*Grannies!* We gotta wait for old Ned—"

"No. Please. Right now. Oh, this is naughty. Let's be—"

A gunshot exploded toward the back of the room somewhere. Men shouted and a woman screamed. Chairs went over, and the sound of breaking glass crashed through the roar.

Wildcat leaped from his chair, almost knocking Millicent to the floor. The sounds were in the back, somewhere near the room where Shipwright was playing chess. Now *what the hell had he done—?*

The crowd had already begun to flood toward the back. Fighting his way, knocking people aside, Wildcat saw that the door to the back room was closed. Somebody in the crowd was trying it, but it was locked.

Forgetting everything but the need to get in there, Wildcat hurtled through the last of the crowd and got to the door. He charged the door, hitting it with shocking force with his shoulder. The door collapsed, splinters flying as it went off the hinges and crashed inside, taking part of the flimsy frame with it.

The force of the charge carried Wildcat careening into the room.

The table was overturned, chess pieces scattered. The window was broken out, blackly vacant against the night of the alley beyond. Simons, his head bloody, lay against the far wall.

Wildcat rushed to him. He was groggy. Wildcat cradled the farmer's head. *"What happened?"*

"Men," Simons grunted. "Dunno—two—three, at least. Through the window—grabbed him—knocked me on the head—took off."

Wildcat whirled. The others were spilling into the room and everybody was yelling excitedly. Wildcat dashed for the window and jumped through it.

He dropped a sickening five feet and sprawled in the black alley, knocking over a garbage can. Climbing to his feet, he looked around. He couldn't see or hear a thing except the noise and light pouring out of the shattered window behind him.

Then, off to the right somewhere, he heard horses. He ran.

He got to the corner just in time to see the clot of horsemen bolt into violent action, heading the other way. At least four of them, maybe five; it was too dark to tell. They rushed down the alley, away from him.

His gun was in his hand, but he couldn't fire. He didn't know who he might hit, and he didn't want to hit the man he was supposed to be protecting.

The horsemen thundered out of sight around a corner.

Wildcat charged after them, hoping to find a horse quickly enough to follow. He ran headlong into some trash barrels and went sprawling, his gun discharging into the sky. By the time he got untangled, the hoofbeat sounds had faded.

Getting to his feet, Wildcat was icily sober. He holstered his gun and started back to claim Freddie and Millicent. The fun, he thought, was over. And Jack Jackson would be fit to be tied.

Ned Shipwright had just been kidnaped.

FOUR

Sticky-eyed from lack of sleep, Wildcat sat in Jack Jackson's office at dawn and listened to Mayor Fred Watts have cats.

"It's all over Redrock by now!" Watts groaned, pacing up and down, his celluloid collar flapping. "In a day or so, it will be all over the country! No one of prominence will ever visit our city again!"

Jack Jackson, as puffy-eyed as Wildcat, glowered from his desk chair. "At the moment, mayor, I'm more worried about the fact that a man might be in danger of getting his head shot off."

Watts' eyes bulged. "They wouldn't do *that*!"

"We don't *know* he's been kidnaped for ransom," Jackson said.

"Oh, but surely they did it for that reason! Surely it wouldn't be for revenge!"

"He wrote a lot of stories, naming a lot of real people," Jackson muttered.

"Oh, *no*!" Watts cried, slapping his forehead. "We'll get a ransom note, I'm confident of that—"

"If he is being held for ransom," Jackson asked coldly, "how are we going to raise it?"

The mayor stopped pacing and stared at Wildcat. "It's all your fault. I should have known better. This is a disaster, a disaster! You shouldn't have left his side! What *right* did you have to sit in that saloon, drinking, while he was in another room somewhere?"

"He was playing chess!" Wildcat shot back. "Izzat such a dangerous thing for a man to be doing?"

"You should have been watching over him! And you had been drinking, I know that—no, don't deny it, I have witnesses—"

"Mayor," Jackson cut in brusquely, "that's enough of that kind of crap."

Mayor Watts stared at him. "Now see here, sir! I—"

Jackson's eyes were hard as he broke in again. "We could have brought in a special deputy from somewhere.

But Shipwright wanted someone like Wildcat, and you jumped at the chance, mayor. Don't deny it. You thought Shipwright would write Wildcat up, write the town up, make us famous. You said so. All right. We did what Shipwright wanted. We did what *you* wanted. Wildcat isn't to blame for what happened. Arguing about that angle doesn't help us, anyway. The thing to do now is keep working on the facts we face right here and now."

"But the town is ruined, ruined," Watts groaned.

"Maybe we can find him fast," Jackson said.

"You said you searched all night."

"Yes."

"You said you're convinced they got out of town with him."

"Yes. We're almost certain. People saw horsemen heading south—"

"Then what chance do we have?"

"Not much," Jackson said bitterly, "as long as you sit here wasting our time with recriminations."

"What would *you* have me do?"

"Get out of here and let me do my work," Jackson rapped.

Watts stiffened. "I shall expect regular reports." He glared, and stomped out. The door slammed behind him.

Wildcat and Jackson looked at each other.

"We," Wildcat said, "are in a pickle."

"Thanks to you," Jackson said angrily.

"You tole the mayor—"

"I told the mayor it wasn't your fault," Jackson shouted. "But let's get a few things straight. You *were* supposed to watch him. You *did* let him go in the other room. You *had* had some drinks. You *did* screw up the whole works."

"But," Wildcat gasped, "like you tole the mayor—"

"I said that because the thing to do now is get cracking on the case. But don't kid yourself, mister! This is your fault!"

"I dunno what I could've done different," Wildcat shot back.

"It makes no difference now. The important thing now is, where do we go from here?"

"I gotta go over to the Hobnob," Wildcat said dully.

His head ached from hangover, excitement, and lack of sleep. "Gotta keep the lady and Freddie calmed down."

"You said Shipwright mentioned threatening notes," Jackson said. "I want you to have that girl search everything in Shipwright's luggage. Clothes. Papers. Everything. Maybe he kept one of the notes. Maybe it could give us a lead."

"Good," Wildcat agreed. "An' you know yesterday, when he got here, I seen some fellers that looked like hardcases hangin' around the depot. I think I'll just have a mosey around an' try to spot 'em again."

"All right," Jackson said, strapping on his gunbelt. "I'm going to take a turn around town, question a few people we missed during the night. Then I'm going to ride out south, across the gorge, just to have a look-see. I'll be back about noon. We can compare notes."

"Jack?" Wildcat said.

The marshal turned. "Yes?"

"You don't think they'd really jus' *kill* ole Ned, do you?"

Jackson's eyes went flinty. "We'd better hope not."

Wildcat left the jail and headed for the Hobnob House. Sweat oozed from every pore, and Wildcat's head felt like a sack of steel shavings. *A man ought*, he thought, *to have some breakfast*.

He decided to wait. Millicent Stork had been hysterical last night. She had acted like Shipwright's kidnaping was the direct result of her moral collapse under the influence of seven shots of redeye whisky. If she hadn't passed out, Wildcat and Freddie might have had to hold her down all night. This was a really lousy situation and nothing could cheer him.

Sure, he hadn't much liked old Ned. Disappointing. But this *was* Ned Shipwright, Wildcat reminded himself. He might be a clown, in person, but he could write; man, could he *write*! There had to be a lot more to him than met the eye. Underneath, he was smart and maybe even tough.

But, Wildcat reminded himself, even if Ned Shipwright was solid horse manure all the way through, he didn't deserve *this* kind of a deal. Ned Shipwright, whatever he was or wasn't, remained a human being in bad trouble.

Most of which, Wildcat thought, *is my durned fault.*

Shipwright had to be found. Fast. Safely.

The Hobnob was like a tomb.

The desk clerk gave Wildcat a frightened glance, but said nothing as Wildcat climbed the stairs. The hallway was deserted. Wildcat rapped on the door of the suite.

Freddie opened it. His face looked like sun-bleached cardboard and he had a wooden bat in his hand.

"Oh," Freddie muttered. "It's you." He let the bat swing to his side.

Wildcat stepped into the sun-drenched room. Wildcat noted that the door to the adjoining room—Millicent's —was closed.

"She okay?"

"Aye."

"Anything happen around here?"

Freddie shook his Neanderthal head, went to the bed, and sat on it, hanging his head.

"We're gonna find him," Wildcat said encouragingly.

The door opened from the other room and Millicent came out. She looked shockingly pale. Her travel suit was gray, freshly pressed, prim, and immaculate. Her hair was drawn back in a bun so tight it appeared painful.

"Have you heard anything?" she asked huskily.

"Well, we're workin' on it," Wildcat said. It sounded lame.

She wrung her hands. "It's all my fault."

"Nay," Freddie said. "It's *my* fault."

"It's nobody's fault," Wildcat said. "It jus' happened."

"I could have helped," Millicent said, her eyes glowing with missionary fervor. "It's my duty to stand by his side, a loyal companion. Instead, I succumbed to evil inclinations of the flesh, debauched myself, and left him in his hour of greatest need."

Good God. "Well, look," Wildcat said. "Jack Jackson has an idea. He wants you to go through everything that belongs to Ned. Notes, books, clothes, everything."

Millicent frowned. "Why?"

"Ned said he'd got a note or two. Threatening notes.

37

Maybe he kept one. Maybe it'd give us a lead."

"I can't go through his effects!" Millicent choked. "It would be like—like a sacrilege!"

"To heck with that. Start right away! It's important!"

"But it would be—it would be as if we were going through *a dead man's effects.*"

"He might be a dead man," Wildcat said, "if you don't get busy."

Millicent looked like she almost fainted, and Freddie flinched. Wildcat gritted his teeth and refused to ease the situation for them. If they were going to function, they had to be shoved into it. He didn't much enjoy the role, but he was the only one available.

"So git busy," he added brusquely.

"Have you *no* feelings?" Millicent cried.

At the same instant, glass tinkled somewhere downstairs. Wildcat spun toward the door. He heard the desk clerk yelling and wheezing.

He was at the door in one stride, just barely ahead of Freddie. They went down the steps side by side, taking them about five at a time.

In the lobby, the desk clerk stood beside the side window, one that looked out onto a dusty alley. The glass was shattered all to hell, and there was a big black rock with a paper wrapped around it there on the floor in the broken glass.

"Did you see anybody?" Wildcat barked.

"No—"

Wildcat heard no more. He was already outside, running across the porch.

The alley looked empty. A glance up and down the street showed no one except the usual loungers and riders. Whoever had thrown the rock had gone down the alley. Wildcat ran.

Behind the Hobnob, the alley intersected another. The alley under Wildcat's feet kept going another fifty yards or so, and then dropped into brush and a gully that marked the end of town. To the right and left there was nothing—the alley curved sharply in both directions.

One chance in three of guessing right.

Wildcat went straight ahead.

Wrong. He plunged all the way to the end of the alley,

and found himself standing in the gully that ended it, out of breath and feeling very much alone. Sunlight filtered through the shabby trees that lined the gully. The dust under his feet was still, protected from wind, and unmarked.

He had figured that the rock-thrower might have ridden this far, then sneaked up. But that had been a bad guess. The man had used one of the other alleys both for approach and escape.

By now, the man was long gone.

Wildcat hiked back to the hotel. He had automatically assumed that the rock with a note attached had something to do with Ned Shipwright. Even Ned had never figured a neater way for kidnapers to let somebody know what the ransom was supposed to be.

This, unlike the guess about the alley, was right.

Freddie and Millicent were back in the room. Millicent was staring at the wrinkled sheet of paper. She handed it to Wildcat with the look of a woman who has just lost her husband and found the insurance had lapsed a day too early.

Wildcat read the note that was smeared, square-printed pencil on yellow tablet-paper:

WE GOT SHIPRIGHT AN IF YEW EXPECK TO SEE HIM ALIVE UGEN, HAVE $5,000 REDDY TO PAY IN 24 OURS. YEW WILL GET ANOTHER NOTE TELLIN YEW HOW TO DEELIVER THE CASH, DO IT ARE WAY OR HE DIES.

Wildcat looked up mutely at Freddie, then at Millicent.

"We'll have to write his publisher," Millicent said hoarsely. "They can have the ransom here immediately."

Thinking furiously, Wildcat agreed. "Okay. But as soon as you do *that*, get back here an' start that search. Understood?"

"For the earlier notes," Millicent said. She was swaying on her feet.

"Yep," Wildcat said. "Hey, are you aw-right?"

"Of course," Millicent said. "I'm fine." And fainted.

The wire to Shipwright's publisher went out before ten o'clock, and within a few minutes Wildcat had Millicent and Freddie back in the hotel, busily searching everything up there in the rooms. Leaving them to the chore, Wildcat did some circulating.

The hardcases he had seen in the depot crowd were nowhere to be found. He even checked the boarding houses and a couple of cot barns. Nothing.

It might be significant, Wildcat figured, *or it might not.* He knew he was grasping at straws, but he planned to keep his eyes peeled. There was a chance—just a *chance*—that they were the ones who had nabbed old Ned.

This train of thought was interrupted by the sight of Jed LaRance snoozing in the hot shade of the Parkley Livery Barn. Wildcat, getting an entirely different idea, hustled over there.

LaRance awoke fast when Wildcat kicked his boot.

"What's the idea?" LaRance growled.

Wildcat grinned and squatted beside him. "I guess you heard how the writer feller got stolen."

"Huh," LaRance said, spitting between his teeth. "Breaks my heart."

"Got any ideas who might of did it?"

"Me?" LaRance demanded, angry. "Hell no, and if I did, I'd keep it to my own self!"

"Stealin' people, you can git hanged for that, ole bud."

"Only if you did it," LaRance spat. "I didn't."

"Got any ideas who might of?"

"You just asked me that. No!"

"You might not like him much, but we need to git him back safe."

"I hope they drop him off a cliff, personally."

Wildcat walked away from him. The question that had motivated the brief visit was pretty adequately answered. Jed LaRance was not the world's best actor; if he had known anything about Shipwright's abduction, Wildcat thought it would have been visible.

Another walk around town turned up nothing. Wildcat checked back at the telegraph office. There was no reply yet from Ned Shipwright's publisher.

Hiking back toward the Hobnob, Wildcat turned the situation over some more in his mind.

He was dead sure by now that Shipwright had been

hauled out of Redrock. If the kidnap gang figured on collecting money, they had to stay somewhere fairly close. They *might* be camped out on the prairie to the north or west, but this seemed unlikely; the camp would be dry, and exposed, as well.

The brush country to the east was more likely; a man could find hundreds of good hiding places out there in the rolling brush. But *south* of town was the best bet of all; there the land quickly became a tangle of wooded hills, gullies, arroyos, dry river ravines, cliffs, and rocky escarpments.

So, Wildcat thought, *they probably were holed up south of the river someplace.*

But that didn't narrow it down much. They could be anyplace out there.

If Shipwright's publisher came through with the ransom money, Wildcat figured, there was a good chance the novelist would be turned loose. Then, eventually, Jack Jackson could get descriptions.

At the moment, however, this all seemed awfully damned slow. Ned Shipwright would not be an easy prisoner. Somebody could get hot under the collar or all liquored up, and kill him as easily as look at him. Maybe Shipwright wouldn't even realize how desperate his danger was. *Maybe he was dead already.*

The thought gave Wildcat chills in the hundred-degree heat. He hurried on to the hotel.

He found Millicent and Freddie going through luggage and papers.

"Find anything?" he asked cheerfully.

"One thing," Millicent replied, handing over a sheet of notebook paper. "I don't know what it means—"

Wildcat took the sheet of paper. It had only one line on it, written in a flowing longhand he assumed was Shipwright's:

gang leader is Donald Keester—Redrock

Tingles down the back, Wildcat read the single line a second time. He looked up; Millicent was watching him closely.

"Millicent, is this ole Ned's handwriting?"

"Yes, of course. Does it make any sense to you?"

Wildcat shoved the note in his pocket and headed for the door. "Keep lookin', an' don't tell nobody about this. I'll be back after awhile."

He took the steps down several at a time, and ran for the jail to see if Jackson was back yet.

Don Keester lived south of town, and was just the kind of guy who would kidnap somebody for $5,000.

Jack Jackson, looking stiff and saddle-sore, was just tying up in front of the jail. He turned as Wildcat approached. Dust sifted in little rivulets off the marshal's clothes.

"I didn't spot anything," he grunted. "Signs in the road too mixed——"

Wildcat shoved the note at him.

"Where did this come from?" Jackson scowled after reading it.

"They found it in ole Ned's durned suitcase or somewhere, Jack."

"Just now?"

"Just now! I come to see if you was back, so we could go together."

Jackson stood there, frowning.

"Well?" Wildcat demanded. *"C'mon!"*

"It doesn't make good sense."

"It says Don Keester! You know he dadblamed well *might* do a deal like this!"

"How would Shipwright know the name of a man planning to kidnap him?" Jackson asked, eyes narrowing further.

"Jack," Wildcat grated, almost beside himself, "I don't know! *Why don't we trot out there an' ask Don Keester?*"

"You're right," Jackson decided. "Let's go."

It was a two-hour ride through the woods and rocky hills going south. The terrain out here was so rugged that a thousand cabins could have been dropped into the woods and no one would have spotted them. It was anyone's guess how many there really were. Even though he and Wildcat both knew the countryside as well as most, they got lost twice on the way to the Keester place.

Don Keester was a widower, about fifty. The wife had

died, the sons had run off, and Keester, a shaggy recluse who seldom appeared in Redrock, was known to skulk around the place with several of his friends who weren't much better. Wildcat had met him a few times; he was a bad drinker, the nasty kind.

The Keester shack was someplace down in a deep ravine, and Wildcat led the way to it after getting lost the second time. The saddle trail through heavy brush, with blackjacks and cottonwoods dense overhead, was so narrow that they went single file, slowly.

"Are you sure this is the right ravine?" Jackson asked.

"Yep," Wildcat said cheerfully. "His shack's up ahead, lessen a mile now."

"Keep an eye out."

"You better believe it, ole bud."

The walls of the ravine looked down on them, providing excellent cover for any guards that might have been set. But no challenges came. Wildcat, all his senses functioning at top efficiency, guessed rather than knew when they were approaching the shack itself, and signaled for a halt. Without a word, he and Jackson tied their horses to saplings. They moved on, then, through the brush, going slowly and picking their way.

Wildcat reached the break in the dense cover first, and signaled the marshal to halt. Jackson crept up beside him and they looked out from hiding together.

The shack, boards and thatch and a few stones here and there, was below their vantage point, sitting precariously on the edge of a mud bank dropping off into the stream that had cut the ravine. Some old barbed-wire fencing was down along one side of the clearing, and a shed near the creek had fallen in.

Cans, paper, broken stumps, pieces of a plow, shattered packing boxes, rotting fenceposts covered the entire area. The shack stood like a tombstone over the desolation, and for a moment Wildcat thought it had been deserted.

Then, however, he spotted a cookstove wisp of smoke from the chimney. He pointed it out to Jackson, who might have spotted it already himself.

Jackson nodded. "I'm going up to the door. Cover me."

Wildcat grabbed his arm as he started to move out. "You might git your tail shot off."

Jackson's lips curled in a thin smile. "If they've got Shipwright in there, we have to fight our way in, anyway. If they haven't, they'll let me stroll right up. This is the way to find out."

Standing straight up, Jackson stepped casually out into the sunshine of the clearing and started for the house at a normal gait, his arms swinging, his hands empty.

It made Wildcat's guts shrivel to watch him strolling toward the shack that way; Wildcat's skin crawled, too, and he felt feverish and exposed.

Glass tinkled in the side window and something spat fire. A bullet *whanged* into space and Jackson leaped sideways, hitting the hard dirt, rolling like a dervish.

Wildcat had no more time to watch Jackson because the attack was on, and Wildcat was hammering slugs into the window and working the lever of the carbine so fast that the empties were hitting each other on the way out. The window imploded under the continuous impact, and curtains went every which-way, and somebody was yelling inside, and through the smoke Wildcat pounded out another half-dozen shots until the hammer hit on empty.

Dropping the carbine, he came to his feet with his six-gun in hand. Jackson was off to the right, having rolled all the way into the creek ditch. Wildcat spotted his head sticking up behind his own gun. For an instant there was total silence. Then Wildcat was charging the shack, running zigzag and firing at the window some more.

The door flew open and somebody ran out. Wildcat stopped firing for an instant.

"Wait a minute! Wait a minute!" the figure yelled hysterically through the roar in Wildcat's ears.

Wildcat pulled up, covering the man. Jackson had come out of the ditch and pulled up in line to cover, too, as another man, then a third, staggered out of the shack.

"Against the wall!" Jackson ordered, swinging the revolver dangerously.

They complied with falling-over-each-other eagerness, leaning forward with their hands against the wall. The first man out had been Keester, potbellied, naked to the waist, bearded, longhaired, barefoot. The other two were contemporaries, no longer young men, thickset. One was bald and clad only in long underwear. The other wore bib-overalls with nothing more in sight, so that his pale arms stuck out against the wall like birdlegs. All three were glassy-eyed and sweaty, as well as filthy.

"I kep' tellin' you to *wait*," Keester groaned, sweat dripping off his nose.

Jackson was going about the business of patting them over for hidden weapons. "When you shoot first, it's late to be telling us to wait, Keester."

"I *tole* you, Don," the man in underwear groaned.

"Shuddup, Steve," Keester shot back.

The one named Steve was currently getting the once-over from Jackson. "We didn't do nothin', marshal! Ast Burt, here."

" 'at's right!" the one in bib-overalls said. "Don said it was on the up-an'-up anyhow, an' then it got all messed up!"

Jackson stepped back from them. "Okay, Wildcat. Check the house."

Wildcat went inside.

The single room was incredibly filthy, and smelled of sweat, tobacco, and whisky. Wildcat completed his survey in moments and went back outside, thankful to draw a breath of fresh air.

"He ain't there, Jack."

Jackson stepped farther back from the three men. "All right. Turn around. But stay close to the wall."

They complied. Keester almost fell down as he turned.

They were drunk.

All three.

Roaring, wild-eyed, stupefied, petrified, falling-down drunk.

"We didn't know it was you," Keester told Jackson imploringly. "All we seen was somebody comin' up on us, an' the sun was bad in our eyes, so I shot once, jus' to check."

"You missed my skull about an inch," Jackson said coldly.

Keester stared, and big tears began to roll down his cheeks. "I *meant* to miss more!"

Jackson held his thumb and index finger close together. "*That* much isn't a very good miss."

"I was jus' checkin', marshal! Honest!"

45

"Why were you on watch?" Jackson demanded angrily. "Why are you all three smashed out of your minds?"

"We was jus' funnin'," Keester hiccupped, still crying.

The one in overalls started crying too. "It won't do no good, Don. Tell 'em."

"Shuddup, shuddup," Keester cried.

"No, no," the one in underwear choked. "He's right. You got us in all this trouble, an' we ain't done nothin'. You gotta tell 'em the whole deal. *Please*, Don!"

Wildcat exchanged glances with Jackson. For a sick instant Wildcat thought they had kidnaped Shipwright and killed him.

Jackson fixed Keester with his eyes. "Tell it," he ordered.

Keester rubbed his hands over his face. "Nothin' to tell—"

"*TELL IT!*" Jackson roared.

"I didn't mean to miss you close," Keester burbled. "I was jus' checkin', honest—"

"What do you know about Ned Shipwright?" Jackson snapped.

"Oh, gawd!" the one in underwear cried. "They *know*, Don! We gotta tell 'em! I don't wanna hang, my momma wouldn't ever speak to me again—"

"*Shup!*" Keester screeched in an agony of apprehension.

For a moment no one spoke. The three prisoners stood there, in various stages of sobbing, with tears dripping off their faces. Wildcat thought Keester had wet his pants.

"All right," Jackson said heavily. "Wildcat, get some rope."

"They're gonna hang us *right now!*" Underwear wailed.

Wildcat knew very well that Jackson had meant rope to tie them for transport into town. But Jackson picked it up instantly.

"And find a good tree," he said.

"Nice one right over there," Wildcat said cheerfully, pointing. "Low limb, real stout."

"No, *no!*" Underwear wept.

"I ain't done nothing," Overalls said huskily, eyes bulging.

Jackson said to Wildcat, "It's too far to bring a horse."

46

"I think we can haul 'em up aw-right," Wildcat said, grinning. "Keester's kinda stout, but with both of us on the rope, we can git his heels up—"

Underwear dropped to his knees, holding his hands up prayerfully. "It was all Don's idea—he had it all worked out with him, he said. We jus' hired on, it was all jus' a joke, see—"

Overalls fell to *his* knees, too. It was sort of pitiful. "Don set it all up—we jus' figgered it was easy money—"

"*Shup!*" Keester cried in desperation.

"We gotta *tell* 'em!"

Keester shook his head. Then he straightened up, trying to pull together something like dignity. "*I'll* tell 'em," he said quietly.

"Tell," Jackson said. By the way his eyes narrowed, Wildcat could tell that Jackson, too, was steeling himself for something bad.

Keester held out his hands, palm up. "That writer feller. He knowed a guy in Kansas City I do, Fred Remmers. You remember him, he ust to live here, he moved up there—"

"I remember him," Jackson rapped. "Get to the point."

"The writer, Shipwright, he writ me a letter. He said he was down on his luck, sorta, he was gonna be around here, he wanted to git stole. He said it'd give him stuff to write about. He said I should kidnap him—steal him, see—an' bring him out here a coupla days, an' then he'd fix it so's you or somebody'd find a clue, an' you'd come rescue him, or else if you didn't, he'd git away hisself, an' he'd git a lot of publicity, an' it'd help him sell a bunch of stories to them magazines an' all, how he got stole an' rescued."

Wildcat couldn't believe his ears. "Shipwright fixed it for you to kidnap him *for a joke*?"

"Not a joke," Keester argued. "He needed publicity, see, an' stuff to write up, an' he said he'd pay us twenty bucks each—"

Jackson cut in. "That's why your name was in his notes, then. He wanted us to find it."

"I dunno about that," Keester choked, on the brink of crying again. "I jus' know it was a nice little deal. I even sent him this pitcher of me so he'd know it was me when I

47

stole him. He writ back an' said later it never come, but he'd know me when I stole him."

Jackson's face was white with rage. "I want to get this clear. Shipwright hired you three men to kidnap him. For publicity."

"That's it!"

"Dirty plucking filligree of a miserable posthole," Jackson said, or similar words. "Don't you idiots know you *broke the law*?"

"We *didn't!*" Keester screamed. "That's just it!"

"Where is he?" Jackson roared back. "Wait till I get my hands on him!"

"*That's just it!*" Keester screamed even louder.

Jackson frowned. "*What's* it?"

"We dunno *where* he's at!"

"You kidnaped him."

"No! We was s'posed to! Only we got in town late!"

Jackson looked like he had just been hit between the eyes with a heavy rock. "What are you telling us now? Where is Ned Shipwright?"

"We dunno!" Keester wept. "We got there—somebody'd already stole him!"

Jackson turned to stare at Wildcat, and for once Wildcat had nothing to say.

Keester and his buddies might have messed up the *bogus* kidnap job, but *somebody else* had done very nicely on a *real* one.

Ned Shipwright had been kidnaped, all right; for real.

And, Wildcat thought, stunned at the implications, *Ned Shipwright probably had no way of knowing the vital difference.*

Somewhere, *somebody* had him prisoner—and he didn't even know it was genuine.

FIVE

Back in the jail office, Wildcat stripped off his sweat-soaked shirt and went to the water bucket for a dipper of refreshment. "I'll say one thing, ole bud. Bringin' in prisoners is hard work, but it beats heck out of gettin' arrested your own self."

Jack Jackson stomped to his desk and dropped into the chair behind it. He said nothing.

"What're you chargin' 'em with, anyway?" Wildcat asked.

"I'll think of a few things," Jackson snarled.

"It don't really sound like their fault, Jack. Shipwright hired 'em."

Jackson glared at him. "Number one: they hired to do an illegal job. Number two: they got here late and let somebody else do it first. Number three: they didn't come tell me about it. Number four: if nothing else will stick, I'll let them cool off a few days on a public drunk charge."

"He was in his own house, Jack!"

"Technicalities!"

Wildcat sighed. "So what do we do now?"

"We ought," Jackson snapped bitterly, "to let the real kidnap gang kill the idiot."

"We can't do that, Jack."

Jackson got to his feet. He stalked to the door, went out, and slammed the door so hard behind him that a picture fell off the wall behind his desk.

Wildcat went to the cot toward the back and stretched out. His head hurt. He knew Jackson. The marshal would storm around town, shouting at people, and work off the worst of his rage. Then he would come back.

Wildcat knew that he should go check on Millicent and Freddie in the meantime, but he was bone-tired. He forced his mind to shut off, closed his eyes, and was, almost instantly, deeply asleep.

It was about an hour later—suppertime—when Jackson woke him by slamming the door on the way in. Sleepily

Wildcat sat up. He felt better. Jackson didn't; not much, anyway.

"Find anything out?" Wildcat asked.

"What would I find out?" Jackson spat.

"Well, did you git an answer from his publisher?"

"Not yet. No." Jackson sat at his desk.

"No second note from the gang that got him?"

"No."

"What're we gonna do, Jack?"

Jackson took a deep breath and leaned back to roll a smoke. He seemed to exert his will to make these calmer movements. "I've got four men deputized. They're stationed around the Hobnob, out of sight but where they can see. When the gang pitches the second note, we'll have a chance to catch them at it. I'm going to eat and go on over there myself. I want you, too."

"Great," Wildcat said cheerfully. "Maybe the publisher'll send us the money by then, too, so's if we don't catch the gang, we can give 'em the ransom."

"I'd hate to do that," Jackson grunted. "But maybe we could try it. Pay them off, get Shipwright back, *then* go after them."

"The thing we gotta do first, Jack, is git him back, an' I don't much care *how*. Do you know he's settin' out there someplace, thinkin' the whole deal is a gag, probably, an' them not even knowin' he thinks that?"

"I know it."

"An' ole Ned ain't exactly the *easiest* person to get along with I ever met, an' he might git irritated, an' start bossin' 'em, an' them git mad, an' him aig 'em on—"

"I know it!" Jackson repeated angrily. "Let's go eat."

"We ought to dig up Millicent an' Freddie, too, jus' in case they've found anything more."

"I just talked to them and they haven't. But let's take them anyhow. The girl is shaken up pretty badly."

"You ask 'em why ole Ned would pull a deal like this?"

"No. But maybe we ought to." Jackson lit his smoke and got up. "Let's go."

The sun was slanting now, and the worst heat of day had begun to ebb. It was only about a hundred degrees, with blowing dust. The brief nap had given Wildcat a fresher outlook, and despite all the problems in the situation, he was anxious to see Millicent again.

It was possible, of course, that Millicent was really the kind of cool-eyed lady she had first impressed him as being, and last night had just been an alcoholic aberration that wouldn't come along again for, say, fifteen years. But Wildcat didn't think so. He had it figured just the opposite: Millicent was all woman underneath that strict exterior, the kind that really turned on, once the fire was lit.

The walk to the Hobnob took only minutes. Both Wildcat and Jackson spotted numerous acquaintances along the way, because this was the time of evening when the shopkeepers came out for air, some of the city workers went home, and the waddies who lived close enough to town for nightly visits were just blowing in. But there were just a few waves, nothing more; you could begin to get the message that people were worried about what had happened. Wildcat sensed that the over-casual greetings made Jack Jackson even more tense.

At the hotel Freddie and Millicent were up in the stuffy room, trying to put together some of the wreckage they had made in their search.

"We figgered you need some grub," Wildcat told them.

"Aye, that's a fact," Freddie said, brightening.

"It's out of the question, I'm too worried," Millicent said.

"Nay, lass, you need to eat," Freddie admonished.

Millicent touched her hand to her hair. "But I look a fright."

"Darlin'," Wildcat soothed, "you've never looked nicer."

She gave him a glance that was supposed to be irritated, but her eyes gave away her pleasure. "Well, I suppose I should *try* to eat."

Jackson said grouchily, "I want to fill you in on where the men will be stationed tonight, anyhow. And there are a couple of questions."

It took Freddie two minutes to get ready, and Millicent fifteen. They went to the Cattlemen's Café and found a corner table.

By careful maneuvering, Wildcat fixed it so he sat next to Millicent. This put Jackson across the table from him and Freddie on his left.

"I just don't know how I can possibly eat," Millicent breathed.

"Well, you can have a little somepin," Wildcat encouraged her.

The man brought the menus.

"I," Wildcat told him, "am gonna have the jumbo steak, rare, with fried potatoes, whatever vegetables you got out there on the side, coffee, plenty of bread an' butter, an' save me a piece of that apple pie."

Jackson ordered the same, with his steak medium.

Freddie ordered brains and eggs, with a side order of grits.

Millicent frowned and put down her menu. "Oh, I guess I should *try*. I'll have the same as you ordered, Wildcat."

The waiter raised his eyebrows. "We got a lady's plate, lady."

"No," Millicent said firmly. "The same as he ordered. And please make sure it's *very* rare."

The waiter went off, shaking his head.

Wildcat moved his knee around under the table and found nothing.

Scowling, Jackson took out a paper and pencil and drew a rough sketch of the Hobnob House and surrounding streets. He put X's where his three deputies would be, where he would be (in the back alley, in a window that commanded a good view of alley intersections), and where Wildcat would be (across the street, in the doorway of the hardware store).

"They'll deliver the second note tonight," he muttered, stabbing the pencil at the crude diagram.

"What's the signal if we see somebody doin' it?" Wildcat asked.

"I've got some of these little rockets left over from the Fourth of July celebration. We'll each have a couple. If there's time, shoot off the rocket. But if there isn't time, just move in and start shooting to attract attention."

"What," Wildcat asked, "if one of your deputies up an' kills the feller?"

"I'm telling them not to shoot anywhere near the person," Jackson said. "That's why I'm in back and you're in front. We can hit what we aim at, and not kill a man by accident."

"It'll be dark, Jack."

"I know that," Jackson said testily.

"We might kill him by mistake."

"It's a small risk, one we have to take."

Freddie asked, "What are *we* supposed to be doing?"

"Just stay in the rooms. With the shades drawn and the doors locked."

Freddie's smashed features wrinkled. "Bloody bad show."

"Why?" Jackson asked.

"I'll . . . tell you later, eh, mate?"

Jackson looked puzzled, but said nothing.

"I s'pose," Wildcat said to Millicent, "Jack tole you how ole Ned had a deal all cooked up."

Millicent's nose went up. "The marshal made some strange insinuations—"

"No insinuations about it," Jackson snapped. "Shipwright wanted a publicity gag. The only problem was, some real people got to him first."

"I just can't *believe* that!" Millicent cried. "Nedwin is such a great artist . . . so—brimming with integrity!"

Freddie sighed. "You might as well be straight with 'em, lass."

"I don't know what you mean!" Millicent said indignantly.

Freddie looked mournfully at Wildcat. "Our boss has been not selling so much of his work the last months. I mentioned it to you before. We didn't know about this thing he had all cooked up, but it wouldn't surprise me none if every bit of it was true."

"Freddie!" Millicent gasped.

"Aye," Freddie murmured. "You see, gents, back a few years ago, Mister Shipwright was one of the first, one of the very first, to be writin' about this West of yours. But others have come along, new writers, new magazines. It's hurt him, some. An' then some folks were saying he had never been west of the Hudson River, he was making it all up." Freddie paused and gave Millicent a hard, stubborn look. "He's been a desperate man."

The waiter interrupted them by bringing the food. Wildcat tested his steaks, and stole a glance at Millicent's. They were rare, all right. The only way they could have been rarer was for the cow to still be alive.

Millicent deftly carved a chunk of blood-red meat and daintily forked it into her mouth.

"The point of the problem now," Jackson said as they ate, "is that the phony kidnap job didn't come off, and we have a real one."

"We still haven't heard from New York," Millicent said.

"The office closes at nine," Jackson replied. "We ought to hear by then."

Millicent frowned. "Publishers are strange. Sometimes they don't work."

"They'd *better* wire that money," Jackson growled.

For a few minutes they ate in silence. Millicent stoked it away like a drover just in off a six-month trail. Wildcat didn't know whether to be pleased or horrified. He had seen women *eat* before, but this was something else.

"Let me ask you, marshal," Freddie said after awhile. "Isn't there a chance of sending out a search party or something and catch the bloody beggars wherever they're holding him?"

"Too much ground to cover," Jackson said disgustedly. "This plan to watch the hotel has to work, or we have to ransom him. I don't see any other way."

"I wish," Millicent said crossly, "we had never come here!"

"About the plan," Freddie said. "You think I ought to, uh, stay in the rooms, you say?"

"You mentioned that before," Jackson said. "What about it?"

Freddie glanced fearfully toward Millicent. She was busy plowing it in.

"Well," Freddie said, his rugged face getting red, "I went out for a bit this afternoon, and I happened to meet this, ah, person."

Jackson looked blank, but Wildcat got it right away. "Hey, Freddie, an' this *person* might have a drink with you, somethin' like that, maybe?"

Freddie looked relieved. "Well—aye."

"Hey, what's her name, ole bud?"

Freddie's ears got fiery red. "Peggy."

54

"Peggy, from the Blue Sky Club?" Wildcat asked delightedly.

Freddie looked at his plate. "Aye."

"Jack," Wildcat grinned, "you wouldn't ask Freddie to stew in his room if *Peggy* wants to have a beer with him!"

Jackson bit his lip. "Damn it, I think Miss Stork ought to have someone with her. I—"

"It's of no consequence, marshal," Millicent said cooly, giving Freddie a dirty look. "I'm quite accustomed to Freddie's night-owl carryings-on."

"Ah, but this is the first time—" Freddie began.

"Don't give them that line," Millicent said wearily. She turned back to Jackson. "I shall be securely locked in. If Mister O'Shea could possibly look in upon me now and then for reassurance, I'll be just fine."

As she spoke, Wildcat felt *bump!* under the table.

"Yeah," he muttered. "I could, uh, reassure her—"

Jackson scowled. "I don't suppose it matters. I'll have a view of the outside windows, and you'll be watching the front, Wildcat. I wouldn't want you leaving your place to go up there, though."

"After we catch the guy, or whatever happens, I could jus' make sure everything is aw-right," Wildcat suggested.

"All right," Jackson said. "You can go, Freddie."

Freddie looked enormously relieved. Millicent cooly continued eating the remnants of her huge steak, and her waxen features showed no hint whatsoever of the nature of the kneesies going on below-decks. Wildcat was perspiring.

The waiter came back to ask about dessert.

While he was taking orders, the old man from the telegraph office scurried in, looked around, spotted Jackson, held up a yellow wire sheet, and hurried across the room.

"It's the reply!" Millicent said.

Jackson got up and went to meet the old man. They exchanged remarks and Jackson took the telegram. He walked back toward the table, reading as he came.

When he reached the table, he was mashed-potato white. He glanced around at them, his eyes at pinpoints.

"Well?" Millicent prodded. Then, when Jackson stared

again at the telegram, she repeated, *"Well?"*

Jackson took a deep breath. "This thing tonight better work. We'd better catch somebody."

Reaching across the table, Wildcat took the telegram. He read:

```
MXFHK87688XZ                    PDNIGHT45783
J. JACKSON U.S. MARSHAL
REDROCK TEX 6899000CFG
```

SORRY OUR AUTHOR MISSING. HE ALREADY OWES US $11,000 ADVANCE AGAINST UNWRITTEN WORKS. CANNOT MAKE FURTHER INVESTMENT IN HIM, SUGGEST YOU CONTACT HIS MOTHER, C/O COUNTY POOR FARM, ZANESVILLE, OHIO.
              T. HERRING, BIG WEST BOOKS INC.

SIX

Scudding clouds made the night black. Standing in the doorway of the hardware store, Wildcat leaned his weight first on one leg, then on the other. It was long after midnight, perhaps after 1:00 A.M. by now, and nothing had happened.

Sunday nights, of course, were always the quietest of the week, and this one had been quieter than usual. By midnight, the few saloons operating openly had closed up. The streets had become nearly deserted, and few lights showed along the rows of buildings. The wind sighed, and off far in the distance a couple of coyotes made lonely sounds. Wildcat was tired and jittery.

From his station he couldn't see any of the other watchers, but he knew where they were.

The hell of it was, of course, that there was no way of knowing when the gang might choose to deliver the next note. The guess that it would be tonight seemed solid. But Wildcat had begun to get the idea that this gang was far from stupid; they were not likely to be trapped easily.

They might, for corn sakes, wait until near dawn, even.

Looking across the street and up at the second floor, Wildcat saw that the single dim light behind shades—the light in the room where Millicent Stork was waiting—still shone evenly. Freddie had shambled off long ago, and if Wildcat knew Peggy, Freddie wouldn't be back until about noon tomorrow. So Millicent was *up there right now*, alone, lonesome, maybe dressed for bed, with her hair down, maybe *in* bed (this hurt), waiting for him; anxious and nervous and wanting him to come on up, and needing him, etc. And here he was, standing in this god-forsaken doorway, with leg cramps, a headache, strained eyeballs, and visions of sugar plums dancing in his head.

The least any decent gang could do was go ahead and deliver their stupid note, and either get captured or get away, so that the rest of the night's affairs could commence.

More time itched into history. The coyotes stopped baying, and a couple of dogs in town someplace took it up. The wind stilled. A few more lights went out, leaving very few still aglow. Wildcat, his eyes fully adjusted to the dense darkness, could make out every storefront and doorway up and down the crooked street, but it was mighty strange to see things like this, deserted, silent, asleep.

It had now been more than twenty-four hours since Shipwright's abduction. Thinking back, Wildcat knew that a great deal had happened. But he felt a pulse of impatience, this time one that had nothing to do with Millicent or any of *that*.

Ned Shipwright, Wildcat thought, probably was more or less safe until this second note got delivered. Then the writer's life would slip into even deeper danger. The longer a gang was together on a deal like this, the more edgy everyone became. Shipwright would be about nine thousand miles from being a model prisoner, and he would irritate them further. This business had to be pushed to some sort of conclusion, and fairly fast. Shipwright might have *some* chance of staying alive another forty-eight hours; beyond that, his life wasn't worth a catskin.

Wildcat watched, and more time went by. He thought about the wire from Shipwright's publisher. It had shaken him up a little. He had always figured Shipwright for a truly great writer, a lot better than Longfellow or any of those guys. It shocked him to think that this great writer's publisher thought no more of him than *that*. And what was the thing about his mother being at a poor farm? *What the hell?*

Feeling some of his idealism slipping, Wildcat bucked himself up. Hell, he had read nearly all of Ned Shipwright's stuff. It was *good,* exciting, colorful; written about guys that were *really* tough. Shipwright knew his business.

He might act funny, you might not even like him much. But underneath he just had to be made of pretty stern stuff, and he had to be smart.

Assuming Shipwright got rescued all right, he was sure to write a book or two about the experience.

Assuming Wildcat was in on the rescue, then Wildcat would be in the book.

Assuming he was in the book, why, naturally he would look good, because, hell, he *was* good.

He might even be the hero.

Wildcat felt a flush of feverish excitement, thinking about that. *Him*, on the cover of the book. *Him*, described and in action. *Him*, saving old Ned. *Him*: a *hero*.

The thought pepped him up so much that he could practically see through buildings, he was looking so hard for the man with the second ransom note. His blood perked faster. This, he thought, was his big chance.

The mood lasted almost an hour, but continued silence then began to dull it quite a bit. He began to get disgusted again. The light still glowed in Millicent's window.

Then, off in the distance someplace, he heard glass break.

Way off, well down the street.

He ignored it.

In a little while he heard voices out behind the Hobnob somewhere. Curious, he nevertheless stood his ground, fidgeting. It might be a trick, and he wasn't about to be suckered. (He imagined the scene in the book: *Despite grave temptation, Wildcat O'Shea stood his ground, his manly features graven of steel in the night of the desert. . . .*)

Then he heard voices around the Hobnob, and Jack Jackson and the deputies walked out into the street.

"Wildcat!" Jackson called harshly. "Come on!"

Puzzled, Wildcat walked out. He saw that Jackson was burned up. "Jack, what's going on? We callin' it off?"

"They delivered the note," Jackson spat, holding out a rock with a piece of paper still tied around it with butcher's string.

"When?" Wildcat gasped. "Where? How? I didn't see a thing!"

"They delivered it," Jackson said, "a few goddamned minutes ago, with this goddamned rock, thrown right through the goddamned window of my goddamned office down the goddamned street."

The note, considerably longer than the first one, was also a little better written. Reading it once through in Jackson's office, Wildcat understood precisely what the gang wanted done—and what a crack it put him and Jackson in.

The money, in silver and gold coin, was to be wrapped up inside a blanket, rolled and turned in at the ends, and then tied with two red bandannas. Jackson himself was to take the "bedroll" down to the depot and get on the last car of the 8:05 train headed south Monday night. Just as the train cleared the far end of the river gorge trestle, he was to toss the blanket roll out on the west side, down the rocky hillside into the brush, as near the semaphore post as he could get it. The note concluded:

Try eny trix an Shipright dys.

Wildcat, alone in the office with Jackson, watched the marshal irritably tack a wanted poster over the shattered window. "So what do we do, Jack?" he asked.

"What do *you* suggest?" Jackson said bitterly.

Wildcat thought a moment. "Well, we ain't gettin' any money from his publisher. Now we ain't likely to catch any of the gang. So I'd say we got two chances left."

Jackson tossed his hammer on the desk and dropped into his chair. "What chances?" he asked.

"We raise the money some damn way an' pay off," Wildcat said, "or we trick 'em an' jus' git ole Ned back safe."

"That narrows it down, then," Jackson said dourly. "We can't raise the money. That's out. Do you have any bright ideas about tricking them and catching them?"

"Well," Wildcat admitted, "nothin' too red hot."

Jackson got up and began to pace angrily. "The years I've put in around Redrock, I don't think I've ever had one like this. A miserable, two-bit novelist from New York comes out here to make fools out of us, the wrong gang kidnaps him, his publisher won't pay for him, the gang throws a note right through my own window, the mayor is having cats, the whole town is upset, we don't have any real idea of what to do next, and we know that if we do the wrong thing, Shipwright is going to end up in some ravine with perforations in that thick skull of his."

"We'll jus' haf to not do the wrong thing," Wildcat said.

Jackson bared his teeth. "Yeah," he said finally.

"At least," Wildcat said cheerfully, "we can figger he's

aw-right now, an' we got till tomorrow evenin' to come up with somepin."

The marshal stopped pacing and took a deep breath. He rubbed his hands over his face, and weariness made his shoulders slump. "I'm keeping the other boys around the Hobnob, just in case. Maybe the best thing to do is what you say: try to get some sleep, try to look at it fresh in the morning."

"Sure," Wildcat grinned. "An' I better go down there an' tell ole Millicent. I'm sure she's real worried."

"Yes," Jackson said sarcastically. "That's a wonderful, humanitarian idea on your part."

"An' then I'll be back here bright 'n' early, an' we can figger out what to do," Wildcat said, heading for the door.

Jackson waved him off in disgust.

Hotfooting it up the street in the dark, Wildcat was a little worried that Millicent would be fast asleep by this time, or out of the whole mood. The light continued to glow in the window, which bucked him up a little. He crept into the hotel, stole up the steps, and rapped gently on the door.

Nothing happened.

Worried, he rapped again.

A soft voice on the other side whispered huskily, *"Who is it?"*

"Me," Wildcat breathed, his pulse leaping.

The door opened. Millicent, wrapped full-length in a somber, dark-colored cotton robe, stood back to let him come in. Her hair was all down over her shoulders in a way that made Wildcat's throat sort of hurt. She smiled wanly.

"I fell asleep," she said throatily.

Wildcat closed the door and quietly closed the bolt. "It's awful late."

Millicent padded barefoot to the couch and sat down. "Has something happened?" Tension had crept into her voice.

"They brang the second note," Wildcat told her, sitting beside her. "We didn't catch 'em, but it's okay; we got a plan all worked out, an' we know ole Ned's aw-right, an' things are gonna be fine."

Millicent frowned with worry. "I was hoping you could catch them."

"Don't worry, honey," Wildcat said, patting her hand. "We'll git 'em tomorrow evenin'."

Her enormous eyes met his.

She pulled her hand away. "Would you like some sherry?"

It sounded like soda pop, but what the hell. "Gee, I sure would. I'm real thirsty."

Smiling, she went to a cabinet and got out a single decanter. She took two small glasses and poured in about enough to wash out your eye with. She brought the glasses back and sat close, partly facing him. She handed over one glass. Their fingers touched in the exchange, and Millicent seemed to breathe very sharply.

Wildcat grinned at her over the glass. "Mud in your eye."

It wasn't bad stuff, real sweet, but definitely alcoholic—which with Millicent was probably a good thing, judging from past performances. However, she seemed very somber, and only sipped from her glass.

"The opportunity to change my life and render service to a man of greatness," she said huskily, "has been something very dear and very meaningful for me."

"He's a good ole boy," Wildcat agreed, his mind not much on the conversation.

"One has to control oneself—control one's feelings—in order to have a life of real meaning and service."

Wildcat put down his empty glass and gently took her hand. It was warm and soft, and he let his fingers steal along her velvet inner wrist. "I know, darlin'," he said.

"All this time," she went on huskily. "*All this time,* I've been true to this calling. It wasn't until I met you—until I let myself have those drinks last night—that I *felt* something again. Do you understand?"

"Sure," Wildcat said, soothing his fingers along her inner arm, reaching the elbow.

Hell, he really did! The poor kid, she had been a dancehall girl or something like that, she had hated it, along had come this dude with fancy talk and big manners and asked her to be his secretary, and she'd had all these kid dreams in her pretty head, and she had jumped at the chance, practically had become a dadblamed nun, and maybe even she had been telling herself she liked it, denying everything else.

But it was inside her all the time, the human side; boy, the side that everybody had, the side that longed for someone, somebody to hold and like and feel and cherish and be really open with—

"I git it," Wildcat replied, aloud.

"I know you don't love me," she whispered. "I know you won't, and I'm not asking that. But I've been alone so long—I've got such a hunger—"

Wildcat reached for her. He did it very gently, because he knew this was no ordinary fun-type thing for her, and he was truly touched.

With a whimper of something like pain she came into his arms, and as she did so, magically, the robe slipped from her arms and shoulders, and she wasn't wearing anything else. *Maybe,* Wildcat thought from a very great distance, *this was not the right place or the right time, and he had to be one of the orneriest guys in the world to be here like this, and enjoying it so much, to boot. But she was very, very beautiful, and every bit as eager in a strangely shy yet knowing way.*

They forgot even to turn off the lantern with its wick turned low in the window before the shade, and it was much, much later—almost dawn—before the flame finally guttered softly and went out.

SEVEN

Mayor Fred Watts wrung his hands as he watched Jack Jackson roll up the blanket containing the bottle caps, spent cartridge cases, and chunks of printer's lead.

"It won't work," Watts groaned. "They'll see through it right away!"

Bent over his office desk, Jackson finished rolling the bundle and reached for the bandanna to start tying it. "They won't know until they get back to their hiding place and unwrap it. By that time we'll have them."

The mayor looked worriedly toward Wildcat, who stood guarding the door against unexpected visitors. "What if O'Shea can't keep up with them after you drop the roll? What if they lose him?"

"Are you kidding?" Wildcat shot back. "Nobody's gonna lose *me*!"

"How can you be so sure?" the mayor parried. "It will be nightfall, and if these clouds stay around, a black night. You don't even know how many of them there might be, or where. They *might* lose you."

"They ain't gonna," Wildcat said.

"They might."

"Nobody ever has, mayor, an' I ain't fixin' to have this be the first time."

"I *wish* there was another way!"

"There isn't," Jackson said, tying the first bandanna, reaching for the other one. "If they have scouts, either here in town or out along the track, all they'll see is me with the bundle. They won't see Wildcat. And when I toss the thing over, it'll be too dark for anybody to see much of anything, especially with the smoke the engine will be throwing back."

Watts snorted derisively. "If O'Shea is dressed like *that*, they'll see him a mile off."

"What's wrong with the way I look?" Wildcat asked defensively. He looked down at himself. He was wearing his green outfit. Everything green. Except his black-and-red striped vest and yellow boots.

"You look," the mayor said, "terrible. Gaudy."

"I'll look nice an' drab for the work tonight," Wildcat retorted. "But it jus' so happens I got a civic duty to do in a little while. I got to take Miss Millicent to dinner."

"It's two o'clock in the afternoon. Isn't that a little late for the noon meal?"

There were two good reasons for taking Millicent out late. One, it was really breakfast. Two, Rita would be having her afternoon nap at 2:30, and thus wouldn't be around to start screaming and throwing things when he and Millicent appeared together.

Wildcat, however, had no intention of explaining any of this.

"There," Jackson said, holding up the bulky rolled blanket. "That's it."

"It will never work," Mayor Watts said.

"It has to," Jackson said.

The southbound night train pulled out of Redrock promptly on schedule. It was a small train tonight. It was, Wildcat thought, probably real nice back there in the caboose where Jackson was. They were probably having a drink and all.

"You comfortable, Wildcat?" the fireman grinned, digging his coal shovel into the pile near where Wildcat was hunkered.

"Dandy," Wildcat grunted.

The fireman, a randy little Irishman, turned and heaved his shovel of fuel into the hotbox. The train was beginning to gather some speed as it moved out of Redrock now. Wind was whipping around in the cab and the coal car, and the fireman had to shout to make the engineer hear him.

"Guess Wildcat got caught with the wrong feller's woman!"

The engineer leaned in from the side window, blinking at a gauge. "Guess this is one way to get your ashes hauled."

"You guys," Wildcat said, "are really funny."

The fireman dug in his shovel again. "How come the black stuff on your face, Wildcat? Some hubby gonna run you alla way to Mexico?"

The engineer tooted the whistle and leaned on the throttle. The train was racketing along now. "Maybe," he said, "all the way to Africa."

Wildcat considered saying something in reply, but decided the hell with it. In his opinion, Jack Jackson's idea of him riding all the way up here was kind of stupid. But sometimes Jackson could be stubborn. The idea was that the pickup man for the blanket roll would be watching the back of the train, so Wildcat, to avoid detection, ought to be far to the *front*. Wildcat had protested having to ride in the damned coal car. But Jackson had started to get a crafty look in his eye, and Wildcat had suddenly had a picture of himself strapped to the cowcatcher. So he shut up.

Now the kidding at least showed no one was onto the gamble. So let 'em have their fun.

It was ten minutes to the far side of the trestle, where the semaphore pole was. Wildcat used the time to check his revolver.

There was no percentage in trying to plan what was now nine minutes up the line. It was all spur-of-the-moment after he left the train, and he had long ago learned that the man who tried to *plan* for this kind of action only ended up in a pickle, because you could never predict what would happen, and prearranged ideas only gummed up your reflexes.

It still seemed a little weird, though, to be rocking along in this coal car, riding into God only knew what. Just forty-eight hours ago, he could remember, everybody had been looking forward to Ned Shipwright's arrival. *I was expecting this big stud with buffalo-hunter hair*, Wildcat remembered. *And there had been all those great dreams of what it would be like to talk—actually talk—with your dadblamed hero, and maybe have him put you in a book. Now, this quickly, the dreams were down the drainhole, and here you were, bouncing holes in your rear end on chunks of coal, riding into somebody's muzzle-blast.*

The world, Wildcat thought profoundly, *was unpredictable.*

Oh, he didn't really dislike old Ned. In his own way the runt had plenty of guts. It was just strange.

The train had reached the level part of its gorge run

where the track hung out on a rock lip. Far up ahead was the faintest glint of a bit of starlight that had leaked through the clouds to shine on the river. The engine was already beginning to strain slightly as the uphill started.

Five minutes, maybe four, to go.

Wildcat stopped thinking about Shipwright. He thought about Millicent instead, which was considerably more pleasant.

The Bible-whappers down in the revival tents, Wildcat thought, *probably would figure he had done a real bad thing to, with, and for Millicent.* Well, he couldn't work up much guilt. She had been radiant at dinner: new color in her cheeks, new lights in her eyes, all gay and dazzling and attentive. It had been a long spell for her, these months of being the uppity secretary, all proper and severe and waxen. Maybe now she would go back to it again, for all Wildcat could guess. But nobody could go on denying their nature forever.

She, Wildcat thought, *had had fun.* So had he. In the quiet, spooky way women sometimes had, she would probably try to start making him think of pots and pans, chintz curtains, and potty chairs. But she was a real lady, with gumption. She wouldn't make a mess of it. She had too much class. She was one hell of a lady, and Wildcat felt a stirring of very deep and genuine affection for her.

The train wheels suddenly got a heavier sound to them, drawing Wildcat back to the business at hand. The train had started out onto the fill that led to the trestle.

Getting up off the coal pile, he stiffly made his way into the engine cab.

"Change your mind, Wildcat?" the engineer grinned.

"Whatever I do," Wildcat said, "or whatever happens, you pay no attention. You got that? You jus' keep this dadburned train headed down the line same as regular."

"What're you gonna do?" the fireman chirped. "Get out and walk?"

The wheels took on the sharply hollow sound that said they were on the long trestle. The train began swaying more as the entire long wooden structure beneath the tracks gave here and there.

Wildcat stepped to the side door of the cab and slid it back. Hanging onto the safety strap, he leaned out slightly and got a faceful of smoke and wind along with a view.

"Close that door!" the engineer said. "A man could fall out!"

Wildcat ignored him.

The engine was about a fourth of the way across the trestle now, the smoke billowing all the way back. Beneath the wheels were open rails and a sheer, empty drop to the river gorge more than one hundred yards below. Wildcat could make out the ugly looking surface of the water.

Peering ahead he could see the far, rocky bank, the point where the trestle was embedded in granite and the track ran up onto solid ground again; cliff-face going up on the left side, loose-fill shale and stubble growth slanting sharply down to the right into heavier brush, and then woods. He couldn't see the metal signal tower yet.

Somewhere in the bullrushes, he thought, one or more guys were waiting to pick up the bundle Jackson would throw from the rear. His job was to go off the coal car past the signal tower and pick up the people as they scrambled for the ransom package. Then he *had to* follow them and break Ned Shipwright out of their clutches. This had to be done fast; once they opened the bundle and found that it did not contain money, as ordered, Shipwright might die at any moment.

Wildcat was sweating heavily. He knew Jackson had sent a man up the line a few miles with a good horse; Jackson would leave the train there, and come back as fast as he could with safety. But that might take an hour or more.

It was up to Wildcat. Jackson might arrive in time to help mop up. That was all.

The train neared the end of the trestle. The engine wheels thudded onto more solid foundations. The incline immediately sharpened and the speed continued to slack off. Looking out the side, but staying back out of sight now, Wildcat could see the steep, rocky drop-off. The train seemed to be going far, far too fast. Only a madman would jump at this speed!

Abruptly the rusty metal braces of the semaphore tower flashed past the open doorway. The rocks were blurring past under the toes of his boots on the door sill. *Too fast.*

He counted off the seconds, calculating how far he *had*

to hang on, to avoid being seen, how soon he *had to* go, or be helplessly out of position.

"Wildcat," the engineer grunted, "will you get out of that doorway? You're making me nervous."

It was now.

Wildcat shoved his gun deeper into the holster, pulled his hat down on his ears, and stepped out into the black.

He hit feet-first, the impact shocking all the way into the base of his skull. The loose shale went out from under him and he plunged onto his back, the rocks tearing him up, and then everything was a blur as he went head-over-heels from his momentum, going down the slope like a ball, telling himself, *Roll up, roll up, stay loose*. He had rushing impressions of train wheels, steam, rocks flying, pain, dirt in his eyes and mouth, crashing through some brush, the tearing of his clothes, a big rock practically smashing his elbow.

Then suddenly he was sprawled in underbrush, spitting dirt and the salt taste of blood.

He rolled over and sat up, dizzy.

Up above his position, fifty or more feet overhead, the last cars of the train chugged by in a cloak of furling smoke and red sparks. The rumble had already begun to abate in the loose earth beneath him.

He hadn't broken anything significant. His hat was gone and so was his knife, but he had hung onto his rifle, and his revolver was still in the holster. Spitting more dirt and blood, he got shakily to a crouching position and looked around.

He had gone all the way down the embankment, ending up in the brush clotting the bottom. He couldn't see much, but off to his left about sixty yards the railroad signpost held up its single, soft green light. The train was almost out of sight, up around the next bend, climbing.

Out near the signal post somewhere, a shadow darted.

Wildcat got to his feet and moved swiftly through the brush in that direction. He ran into an old coil of rusty barbed wire, and had to detour, losing all sight of his man while he did so. But when he came out on the other side, going to his belly for a look-see, he got a perfectly clear view for an instant of his shadowy prey standing spread-legged on the slippery rock slope. The man was tall, but nothing else could be seen.

Wildcat stayed where he was, fighting to keep his breathing quiet. He was about twenty-five yards from the man.

A voice more distant—down to the left in the brush—shocked him. "It rolled that way, Johnny."

"Yeah, yeah, I know," the figure on the slope replied. Then it moved nearer Wildcat.

"Right in there, I think."

The man on the slope bent over and picked something up. Against the faint light of the cloudy night sky Wildcat could make out the outlines of the blanket roll.

"I got it."

"C'mon, then. Let's get outta here."

The man went down the slope, his back partially to Wildcat. Seeing his general direction, and knowing about where the other voice had come from, Wildcat bellied into the brush on his left and began crawling fast.

If they were on foot he could follow them all the way in. But he had to stay close in case they had faster transportation.

Clawing through the weeds and stickers, Wildcat heard the two men talking ahead, but he couldn't make out their words. They seemed to be sauntering on down the more gentle incline, deeper into the woods. Then he got a glimpse of their shadows up ahead in the brush, walking side by side. The tall man still had the blanket roll under his arm. The second man, smaller, was carrying a rifle or scattergun.

With their backs to him and the gap beginning to widen, Wildcat had to take the chance of getting to his feet and following more rapidly, moving from tree to tree.

"Didn't see anything, did you?" one of them asked the other.

"Nothin'. I'd say Lederer figgered it perfeck."

"I was worried, man."

"Well, we got it now. All we gotta do is report back, split the money, git rid of him, an' hightail."

"Izzat roll heavy?"

"Plenty heavy." The man laughed.

By this time they had reached the more level floor of

the woods, well below the railroad right-of-way. The two men walked confidently, being careless. Wildcat managed to get closer—close enough so he could hear their labored breathing.

Up ahead of them two big shadows moved around, and Wildcat heard the nickering of horses. He felt a pulse of irritation. Really, it had been too much to hope that they would stay on foot. He had hoped for it anyway. Now he had to make a move or be left behind. He darted nearer them, moving with confident silence in the dry brush.

The men reached the horses. They untied the reins from trees and moved their mounts around to climb aboard. Wildcat delayed, slipping a few paces closer. He had to be sure there wasn't a third man as guard.

The smaller man swung up into the saddle. "Let's git outta here."

There was no third man.

Wildcat moved.

He was halfway to them before they caught his movement, and then it was the horses that caught it first, rearing up and nearly upseating the smaller man who was already in the saddle. The tall one staggered back as his animal plunged nervously. Wildcat, running all-out, closed on the big man as he began to turn. Wildcat's rifle butt swung in a tight arc and hammered into the side of the man's skull, felling him.

The man in the saddle cursed hoarsely and tried to swing his shotgun around. Wildcat leaped over a stump and caught the man's arm, twisting it savagely. The gun flew and the little guy spun out of the saddle. He hit, rolled, and tried to scramble to his feet.

Wildcat shoved the muzzle of his rifle into the man's face. "*Don't*, buddy!" he ordered.

The little man's close-set eyes glinted with shock and fear. "What do you want? What's—?"

Wildcat risked a glance to make sure the taller man was out cold. He was. Wildcat returned his attention to the one in front of him. "Kick that scattergun farther away." The gun clattered in the dirt. "Aw-right. Now ease your iron out of the holster slow an' easy, an' drop it."

With his partner stone-cold and the muzzle of a Winchester repeater about an inch from his nose, the little man obeyed very carefully. He looked scared, badly.

Jerking a rope off one of the saddles, Wildcat lashed the little man's hands and feet, hog-fashion, and just to be sure, stuck his bandanna in his mouth. The man choked and strained to no avail. Wildcat did a more careful job of tying and gagging the unconscious man, the one who had picked up the blanket roll.

Wildcat then dragged the unconscious man up to the nearest large tree and propped him in a sitting position. His bearded face was still slack and he was out to the world, but his breathing was steady and he wouldn't choke in this position.

Going back to the little man, who was still struggling, Wildcat jerked the gag out of his mouth.

"I dunno who you are," the little guy spluttered, "but you can't—"

"Shut up," Wildcat panted, "an' listen."

The man glared, but he still had too much fear in his eyes to make it convincing. He kept quiet.

"We're gonna git on these horses," Wildcat told him quietly, "an' you're gonna take me to where you got Shipwright."

"Like hell! I—"

Wildcat gently thumbed back the hammer of the Winchester, which he again had leveled on the man's face. It wasn't a *big* sound, comparatively, but it had a magic effect. The little man made a strangling noise and stopped talking very suddenly.

"You," Wildcat told him, "are gonna do what I say."

"Yessir! Yessir!"

"Where at have you got Shipwright?"

"Don't shoot! I'll tell you!"

"Tell."

"Down back thataway—west an' a little south. A box canyon. You go down across the road an' past a funny-lookin' hill that looks like the top got lopped off—"

"How far?"

"About five miles."

"This side of the river bend?"

"Yessir!"

Wildcat dug a stub pencil and scrap of paper out of his

72

black vest. Using one of the saddle fenders as a smooth surface, he printed a note:

JACK—DOWN IN A BOX CANYON, DOWN PAST STUDSTELL'S SOMEPLACE, PAST FLATHEAD ROCK, THIS SIDE OF THE RIVER.

At this point he remembered something. He looked hard at the little man, whose eye-whites gave away his terror. "How many of you?" Wildcat asked.

"Five of us."

"Countin' you an' this other feller?"

"Yessir."

"You stayin' in a line shack, or what?"

"A cave."

Wildcat added this information to his note, took the paper over, and used a twig in a buttonhole to pin it to the unconscious man's shirtfront.

Jack Jackson would be here in a couple of hours. He would be looking hard. Wildcat felt confident the marshal would find this man propped up here. The note would save a hell of a lot of time.

Wildcat knew, however, that he couldn't wait for Jackson. The men back in the canyon would have the trip timed. If hours passed, and the messengers didn't return, they would tumble to what was going on.

Wildcat turned back to the little fellow. "I'll tell you what we're gonna do. I'm gonna untie your legs, an' then tie your hands to your saddle horn. You're gonna take me to that cave."

"If I do that, Lederer will kill me!"

"Buddy, you don't have much choice."

"*Listen!*" the little man wept. "You don't *know* them guys! Johnny an' me, we're in it, but we're just hired on. Lederer an' them other two—that Bus an' Rick Bragg—they'll *kill* me!"

The names meant nothing to Wildcat, but his captive's terror was meaningful. He was not waltzing into something likely to be easy.

Using the unconscious man's knife, he cut the leg ropes on the little man and then went ahead to free him and put

73

him on the horse. He retied the man's hands on the saddle horn.

"You lead the way," Wildcat instructed. "Jus' figger on one thing: from here on out, it's me or the rest of you. If you try somepin funny, I jus' ain't gonna have time to mess around with you."

Looking down at him from the saddle, the little man shuddered and said nothing.

Wildcat gagged him again, tied the phony blanket roll onto the back of the other horse, climbed into the saddle, sheathed the rifle, and took out his hand gun. He leveled it on his mute captive.

"Aw-right, ole son. Lead the way," he ordered.

Awkwardly using his fingers on the reins, the little man turned his horse and started into the wood, heading west and slightly south. Wildcat touched his heels to the flanks of the big gelding under him and stayed close.

The ride took them along a faintly worn path, through heavy brush, across about a mile of open hillside grassland, and then into the tangled, rocky jungle of the canyons and ravines. Wildcat kept very close to his captive. Overhead, against the black hulks of hills, the night clouds began to break up here and there; a few stars peeped through.

Wildcat had not pressured for additional information about the lay of the land ahead of them. He had pushed his luck—and the other man's fear—about as far as possible, so far, he thought, he had accurate information. At any point beyond this his captive might have begun to think a little, and to spout lies that would be more harmful, possibly, than no information at all.

From here on out, it had to be taken as it came along.

His captive continued to slant southwesterly, taking them past the Studstell property farther south than Wildcat would have guessed. He wondered how far Jackson would miss the route. But in another little while they rode fairly close in under the flat-topped hill that everyone in the area knew as a local landmark; then Wildcat's worries about Jackson finding the way began to ease again.

By now Wildcat's body had begun to cool from the exertion and nerves of the train jump and brief struggle. He was stiffening up. He had banged his left elbow a bad one, and it sent pains up into his shoulder. Somewhere along the line he had opened a deep gash in his forehead. It had stopped bleeding by now, but the caked blood was stiff and uncomfortable, studded as it was with bits of dirt and rock.

None of this was of much consequence. More minutes passed, and their path descended through a small creek and then farther down into the opening of a long, rock-walled canyon. It appeared to be a mile long, or more, and far up ahead could be seen more walls against the cloud-scattered sky.

They had reached the box canyon.

It was narrow, the walls not more than two hundred yards apart, a small dry branch running along the bottom. The horses walked through waist-high grass most of the time, occasionally encountering brambles. Peering up at the wall of the cliff on his right, Wildcat could make out the black sockets of many small, windhewn caves. It was one like this, he guessed, that they were headed for.

They rode along another five minutes or so, reaching denser woods in the floor of the canyon. Beginning to feel the pressure more intensely, Wildcat rode up alongside his prisoner and tugged the reins to a halt.

Standing the horses, he leveled his gun on the man and pulled the gag out of his mouth.

"Whisper," he instructed softly. "How much farther?"

"Right up ahead," the man choked, dry-mouthed.

"Where?"

The man pointed with his tied hands. "We slope off to the right. In that clump of cottonwoods. We tie up there. We go up the slope—see there where the rocks hang out?—and the cave is in there."

"I don't see a light."

"They's canvas tied over the hole that goes in."

"Is there a guard?"

"I don't think so. Never has been."

Wildcat jammed the gag back in his mouth and told him, "Do jus' what you an' Johnny'd be doin', comin' back. I'll jus' foller you."

They rode forward at an easy walk. Crossing a slight,

open area where the creek puddled and still held water, they moved on into the cottonwood grove. The big trees closed over their heads, making it dense black. Sweat trickled into Wildcat's eyes and stung.

Suddenly they reached a small, partially cleared area under the trees. Just ahead, several strands of rope had been drawn from tree to tree, forming a small corral. Inside the roped enclosure several horses nickered and moved around. Wildcat could make out a hanging branch-fence between two of the trees, and some saddle gear piled up under a canvas.

"Aw-right," he muttered, reining up.

He swung out of the saddle, got the blanket roll under his hurt arm, and moved forward to the other man's horse. He slashed the ropes binding him to the saddle and motioned him down.

The little man swung stiffly to the ground.

"Put 'em in," Wildcat ordered quietly.

His prisoner hobbled forward to the makeshift gate, lowered it, and herded the two horses inside. It crossed Wildcat's mind that it might look more normal to unsaddle them first, but he decided that two men returning with thousands of dollars in ransom money wouldn't bother just yet. He motioned his order, and the man put the gate back up, hanging it on tree nails.

"Take me up," Wildcat whispered.

They went around the corral, under the trees, and out the other side. Here the ground vaulted up sharply, becoming barren. The rocky slope went up perhaps fifty yards of boulder-strewn climbing, then appeared to level off under the huge, overhanging granite ledge that Wildcat had seen from a distance. It was, Wildcat had to admit, a great natural fortress.

The little man started trudging up the incline. Wildcat followed, his gun partially hidden under the blanket roll. Their boots crunched loudly on the loose rocks and chips.

Wildcat knew just how desperate this gamble had now become. The idea of climbing up, open like this, to a *cave*—well, it was more than he had bargained for. He had expected an open camp, or a shack; either of these could be slipped up upon.

They walked up past some big boulders which appeared

to hang by threads. Turning past them, the little man started along a shelf leading to the flat area under the overhang, and as Wildcat let his eyes slip ahead, he spotted for the first time the tiny sliver of light which revealed where a canvas was over the hole to a cave. It was about thirty feet away, and he marveled: no guards, no one coming out to challenge, or even ask if the delivery had been made?

The little man stopped dead, and Wildcat almost bumped into him.

They were standing right beside a gigantic rock formation that loomed ten feet over their heads.

In this instant several items congealed in Wildcat's brain. The approach without a sentinel. The walk up without a challenge. The sounds of their coming, with no one opening that cave flap to yell down with curiosity. The quiet. Now, the little guy stopping so fast.

Trap, Wildcat thought.

When in doubt, attack. He knocked the little man sprawling and took the first step in a direct, charging line for the mouth of the cave.

But in this instant some pebbles crashed down on his head and shoulders from the rock formation overhead, and he just managed to catch the sight of something big—a man—coming over the formation to jump down on top of him.

He *tried* to move fast enough—*how* he tried. But the loose rock underfoot betrayed him and he slipped, and then the man's great weight shocked down onto his back and shoulders, spilling him forward on his face, and then, *oh boy, did that hurt,* and then—

Nothing.

EIGHT

For hiding, it was a great cave. For being a prisoner, it was awful.

Somehow nature had knocked only a small, circular hole in the wall of the cliff, one about four feet in diameter, but then the wind or water or something had gouged out a much bigger cavity inside. The cave was about fifteen feet wide, and tall enough toward its front for a man to stand with plenty of head-room to spare. The moist sandstone walls and roof tapered back into the cliff slowly, like a funnel, coming to a black point perhaps thirty-five feet inside. This rear portion tapered slightly uphill, and there was a crack back there somewhere, a natural chimney.

Blood in his eyes again, Wildcat crumpled against a side wall of the cave, pretending he was still out cold. Through the gore on his face, however, he had studied the situation carefully.

The fire was rather near the front and was fed from a little pile of twigs nearby. A canvas affixed to the entrance with nails into the soft rock kept light from leaking out. A lantern standing on the dusty cavern floor near Wildcat provided most of the light. In the back, where the roof tapered, the gang had cached its supplies and bedrolls.

Near the far wall, sitting up, hands and ankles tied, was Ned Shipwright. He was brightly awake and looked angry. His coat had been torn up and he was covered with rock dust and sand. One of his eyes was black and swollen.

Only two of the gang had been in the cave when Wildcat woke up. He had figured out their names. The one spooning coffee into the scorched porcelain pot beside the fire was named Rick. He was tall and lank, with sunken cheeks that his skimpy black beard did not fill, and had an extra gun belted on his left side. He looked like a real hardcase, but he didn't interest Wildcat as much as Lederer did.

Lederer moved back and forth in the cave, big hands clamped behind his back, his shaggy, blond head down in deep thought. Each time he walked over the spread-out blanket roll, he sullenly kicked at the collection of junk that had been packed in it instead of ransom money. Lederer moved with the hulking grace of a mountain cat. He looked about forty, maybe older, he wore tattered clothing like a mountain man, he had to weigh 250 pounds with his six-foot frame, and he had hands like big sirloins.

Wondering where the other men had gone, Wildcat tried to figure some plan of action. He couldn't come up with anything. He continued to play possum.

In a little while Lederer stopped pacing. He watched Rick panning water from a bucket into the coffee pot. "Rick, splash a little of that in this 'un's face."

Rick looked up, dubious. "I hit him hard, boss. I don't think—"

"Try it anyway. I got to question him."

Rick got stiffly to his feet. Wildcat peeked a glimpse of him coming over with a dipper of the water, then squinched his eyes tight.

The water shocked against his face, dousing his chest as well. He gasped involuntarily and then made a big thing of groaning and kicking a little, like a man regaining consciousness.

Lederer didn't give him time to finish the act.

A hand grabbed Wildcat's hair and jerked his head back savagely. Wildcat opened his eyes and saw Lederer staring down at him from a crouching position. Wildcat tried to pull loose, but Lederer only hauled his head back more sharply, banging him into the rock wall.

"All right, O'Shea," he said. He had a high, unpleasant voice. "What was your plan?"

"I dunno what you mean," Wildcat said.

Lederer's right hand smacked hard across his face, making stars fly. "You came waltzing up here with this blanket full of trash. Where are the rest of your people? What's the plan?"

Salt in his mouth, Wildcat considered how nice it would be to get loose for about six seconds. He held his temper. "We didn't have no more than this. We—"

Lederer's opened hand shocked across his mouth again.

Wildcat gasped, "They threw the money off, or whatever it was. All they tole me was to try an' foller you all, an' make sure Ned didn't git hurt."

"There was no money in that blanket. You know that."

"I dunno anything! I jus' done what they tole me!"

"Teddy said you pinned a note to the front of Johnny's shirt after you propped him up. Who was the note for?"

"I figgered somebody'd come along—"

Lederer made an angry, jerking motion with his hand which banged Wildcat's head back hard against the rock wall again. Then the gang leader got to his feet, fuming, and pointed down.

"Listen, O'Shea. I sent Teddy back with Bus to get Johnny. You'd better hope the three of them get back here in a little while. They're moving real careful, and if they catch sight of a posse out there anywhere, you and this lousy writer aren't going to be alive to tell anybody anything by the time they find you."

"I say!" Ned Shipwright piped up irritably. "This bloody charade has proceeded quite far enough!"

"Keep your mouth shut!" Lederer snapped.

"You've done quite enough," Shipwright insisted. "My man is here, and it wasn't necessary to injure him in this manner. Now free both of us at once! I insist!"

Lederer's flat features became thoughtful. "Rick, untie him a few minutes."

"That's a good man," Shipwright said, brightening.

"You can stand up and move around a little," Lederer told him. Then he added, "Rick, if he tries anything again, knock him out again."

"I told you," Shipwright retorted angrily, "that you can now free us."

Lederer moved like a panther across the cave and stabbed an index finger into Shipwright's chest. "Shut —Up," Lederer grated.

Eyes wide with shock, the writer said nothing.

He was a hard man to convince, Wildcat thought. *He was so damned well filled up with himself that he still hadn't tumbled to the fact that this kidnap job was the real thing.*

Wildcat envied him his ignorance. The entire gambit had gone sour. There was no way to estimate how long the drygulching on the hillside had put him out of awareness, but he guessed it was about an hour. If Lederer had sent the little guy and another man back to reclaim Johnny right away, they would be returning fairly shortly. Then it would get worse. Wildcat had more than a sneaking suspicion that Lederer was now only waiting for the other men's return before deciding precisely what to do next.

The options did not look good. Lederer was both worried and angry. He would get out of here quickly. There was a faint possibility that he would move his prisoner to another hiding place, and send one more note in a last effort to get the $5,000. But, even in this event, Shipwright would be the only prisoner moved, and that left Wildcat O'Shea either abandoned here, probably to starve, or tossed down a gorge somewhere along the line.

The only other alternative that Wildcat could see was even worse. That one had them killing both him and Shipwright on the spot, and high-tailing it.

He watched the man named Rick untie Shipwright's hands and feet. The writer got painfully to a standing position and hobbled around, rubbing his wrists. Wildcat noticed that his fingers were blue, and felt a stab of pity. Shipwright's clothes were torn up, he was covered with dirt, he had been beaten up. But he still maintained that stubborn air about him, a mixture of outrage and sheer arrogance.

Lederer turned back to Wildcat. "You should have sent the money. It would have been a whole lot simpler."

"An' then let you kill him anyhow?"

Lederer spat. "We had it worked out. Were going to ride him up near the train line and leave him all in one piece."

"An' have him tell us what you look like, an' us be right after you?"

"We would have split, would have been so far away by then that you'd never spot hide nor hair of us."

Wildcat wondered where Lederer was from. He wasn't a Texan; you could tell that by his accent, which was rounder, not exactly more southern, but with less twang.

"We tried to raise the money," Wildcat told him honestly.

"You couldn't?" Lederer's face twisted slightly with surprise.

"Redrock ain't exactly the richest town in the world."

"The people that publish his books—"

"Tole us he already owed 'em eleven thousand, an' sorry."

Ned Shipwright, who had been flexing his legs painfully, snapped to attention. "You wired my publisher?" he asked hotly.

"Hell, yes," Wildcat retorted.

"They sent the money, of course! Where is it?"

"They said," Wildcat told him, "to try your momma at the poor farm."

"That's a bloody lie!" Shipwright started for Lederer, brushing past the startled Rick. "Now see here, my good man!"

"Get back over there and shut up," Lederer growled.

"I will not *tolerate* further beastly behavior!" Shipwright cried, and hit Lederer in the chest.

It was a crazy gesture, one of sheer, childish rage, and didn't even make Lederer blink. But his response was instantaneous. The gang leader swung with brutal power, his fist crashing flush onto the smaller man's chin. Shipwright shrieked, was propelled backward across the cave, hit the wall, slid to the floor, and lay there, not moving.

"You didn't haf to do that," Wildcat said angrily.

Rubbing his fist, Lederer turned and looked down at Wildcat. "Is that a complaint? I don't like complaints."

Wildcat chilled. Behind the flatness of Lederer's voice and the waxen plains of his face was something else: a suddenly unmasked cruelty that had nothing to do with rage or any other emotion.

Lederer liked to kill.

Wildcat managed a grin. "I ain't complainin'."

The big man stared down at him another long minute, still rubbing his fist.

The moment passed. Lederer's barrel chest heaved with a deep breath. "They wouldn't send the money, you say."

"They sure wouldn't."

Lederer turned to look down coldly at the unconscious Shipwright. "Ever since I saw him up in St. Louis, I figured he was the perfect mark. Then when I got this set up, it started off *too* good. He didn't raise a hand against us when we grabbed him. Then all this funny talk. Didn't make sense."

Perhaps, Wildcat thought, *honesty would be the best policy.* "He don't know," he said, "because he figgers this is all a gag."

Rick straightened up from the fire. "A *what?*"

Lederer's eyes narrowed. "How come would he think that?"

"He's been down on his luck. We sent that wire to his publisher, they sent us back one saying he already owes 'em all that money. He's been writing bad, or not writing at all—I dunno. This trip out here, the whole thing—maybe even the speech-making in places like St. Louis an' Kansas City—are to git money. He's *broke.*"

"But you said he thinks this is a gag."

"He had it fixed up with a bunch of guys here in Redrock, they was s'posed to kidnap him, only not for real, you understand, an' keep him a coupla days, an' then either let him escape his own self, or leave me a bunch of clues so's I could git him."

Lederer rubbed his eyes. *"Why?"*

"Git him a bunch of publicity," Wildcat explained.

Lederer unleashed a torrent of profanity. He stomped up and down the cave, kicking things. "No wonder he acted like he did! You mean he thinks we're his *hired* gang?"

"That's what I figger."

Rick paused in the act of pouring coffee, his eyes wide. "That's why he mouthed at us the way he has. Hell, he don't even know what's going on."

"Shut up, shut up," Lederer snapped. "I have to think."

He walked up and down, his face working. "He's broke? He's got no money, or not much? His publisher won't pay off? He thinks it's all a stunt?"

"That's gospel," Wildcat said solemnly.

"Where do *you* fit in?"

"Well, after you grabbed him—"

Sounds outside broke off his statement. Rick, grabbing a rifle, scrambled to the entrance and vanished past the loose-hanging canvas. Lederer, a gun appearing as if by magic in his right hand, moved to the doorway and crouched in it, waiting tensely.

Distantly, a voice came from outside. "Red River."

Then, nearer, Rick's voice. "Come on up."

had only two or three to get ready, at the most, since his and Teddy's would still be saddled from their fruitless trip to retrieve Johnny.

Wildcat had been working on the ropes around his wrists all the time, trying to stretch them or rub them against the rock wall, but he couldn't tell whether he had accomplished anything. He was helpless.

They would finish clearing out the cave. Then they would all go out, all but one. That one, probably Lederer, would stay behind just long enough to put a bullet in Wildcat's brain.

Where in the hell was Jack?

The moment the thought crossed Wildcat's mind, he knew it was a futile hope. Jackson had evidently collected Johnny and put him somewhere else. Fine. But Jackson was working alone, and had to come across country, groping in the dark. Only a miracle would get him here in time.

Wildcat strained at the ropes so hard that his shoulders cracked.

Lederer crouched beside the dead fire, drawing a diagram in the dirt with a stick. "We'll go out the end and reach the river bottom," he explained to Rick. "You up front, watching close. We'll have Bus come along like in drag, maybe a quarter-mile back. That puts me and Teddy with Shipwright in the middle. You follow the river bottom where it curves along like this. I've been over that route and it's clear. We'll move as fast as we can. You keep pushing it. If you spot anything, you double back and let us know."

Rick scowled at the diagram drawn in the rock-dust floor. "How far?"

"Till daylight, anyway. Then we'll see."

"We'll never be able to slip back into town an' deliver another note."

"We don't have to," Lederer grunted. "Shipwright has some money someplace. We're going to lay low and keep right on going south. In a day or two we'll be holed up good someplace in the mountains. Then we make Shipwright tell us where his money is. Then one of us goes and gets it and brings it back."

"What if he won't tell us?"

Lederer's jaw set. "He'll tell us."

86

"He might not have much."

"We'll take what we can get!"

"If it's in a bank—"

"We'll make him write us a draft, and we'll go cash it."

Rick shook his head. "I don't like it."

"It's that," Lederer said, "or just kill him right here and now, and get out of here with nothing at all."

Rick nodded grimly. "Okay. I guess we got to try it."

Teddy hurried back in, panting, and got his second load. He hauled it out.

Lederer spat. "Help Teddy. He's taking too damned long."

Rick moved to the back of the cave, got an armload of blankets, and went out with them. Lederer crouched by the fireplace, frowning at his diagram in the dirt.

From outside, a voice called, *"Boss?"*

Lederer looked up, hawklike. "What?"

"Do we leave Johnny's horse, or what?"

Cursing, Lederer stood and moved to the canvas flap. Pushing it aside, he left the cave. His voice came back distantly as he went down the rocky slope, muttering.

Alone now with only the unconscious Shipwright, Wildcat hurled himself into the job of sawing his tied wrists against the wall. But the ropes wouldn't give an inch.

Across the cave Ned Shipwright opened his eyes, sat up. Stunned, Wildcat stared at him.

Shipwright brushed off his arms and vest. "I've jolly well finished this stupid farrago," he said conversationally. "Under no circumstances will I allow it to continue."

"Cut me loose!" Wildcat hissed. *"Cut me loose, quick!"*

Shipwright gave him a scornful glance. "Really, do we have to indulge in these theatrics?"

"There's a knife by the fire," Wildcat said urgently. "Quick!"

Shipwright, continuing to dust himself off, walked painfully over to him. "Oh, by Jove, they have bound you, haven't they? This is insane. I'll never again hire a man without a complete background investigation."

"Cut me *loose*, Ned, goddam it!"

Shipwright strolled to the fireplace, picked up the knife, came back, knelt stiffly, and sawed through Wildcat's leg

87

ropes. "Lean forward, old man. I daresay you might resent it if I should cut your wrists by mistake."

In an agony of haste, Wildcat obeyed. He felt the cold blade slip between his wrists and saw at the ropes. Suddenly they parted.

"There," Shipwright sighed. "Now I suggest we—"

Wildcat heard the sounds of boots on gravel just outside the cave. *"Git back over there an' ack like you're still out cold!"*

"Really, O'Shea, I—"

"Do it!"

Something in Wildcat's tone got through. Shipwright stared at him, then wordlessly scuttled back to the other side of the cave and dropped into a position similar to the one he had been in earlier.

Just as Wildcat stuck his own hands back behind his back, the canvas flap swept back and Lederer came in with both Teddy and Rick behind him. Rick paused and jerked the flap off its nails, showering stone fragments.

"Get it out, get it out," Lederer said impatiently.

Teddy and Rick scrambled out with the last of the supplies. Only the lantern and some trash remained in the cave. Lederer looked around.

Bus came into the entrance. "Hosses ready."

Lederer thumbed at Shipwright, who was making a good imitation of being out cold. "Haul him out. Get saddled. I'll take care of this other one."

Bus went over to Shipwright and reached down toward him. Wildcat didn't know whether he intended to slap his face or try to pick him up. Wildcat was watching Lederer, waiting for the man to turn even slightly so there would be some chance of leaping at him, trying to get one of the guns.

But then, shockingly, Ned Shipwright went into action.

As Bus leaned over him, Shipwright suddenly stiffened and reached out, calmly plucking Bus's revolver from his holster.

"Hey!" Bus yelped.

Squinching his eyes and holding the revolver at arms' length with both hands, Shipwright thumbed back the hammer and let go.

The explosion was astounding inside the cave. Shipwright fired the gun again, trying to hit Bus, maybe, or possibly Lederer, but shooting all over the place. Wildcat had a frozen split-second view of Shipwright grimly holding the gun out, aiming with one eye closed, and being about four feet off-line on either man. The gun banged a third time with shocking quickness, and bullets were bouncing all over the place, rocks falling, smoke coming up, Bus staggering backward in shock.

Wildcat didn't have time to see any more. He was on his feet, headed for Lederer, who had spun to face Shipwright. Wildcat hit him with his shoulder, driving him into the far wall.

"Come on!" Wildcat yelled at Shipwright. "Let's git outta here!"

Shipwright jumped to his feet, accidentally firing again as he did so, and the bullet hummed wickedly past Wildcat's ear and then hammered into the ground beside his left foot on the rebound. Wildcat grabbed the gun out of Shipwright's hand and swung it bluntly into Bus's skull, felling him.

Then, grabbing Shipwright by the collar, he charged for the cave mouth.

They went through together, staggering out onto the loose rock of the slope. Down below, somebody yelled and fired up at them. Wildcat slung a shot back down the hill in reply, and was gratified to hear someone yelp and go down.

There wasn't time for anything else. The path off to the right—downhill and toward the brush—looked open. Grabbing Shipwright by the vest, Wildcat tore down the slope as hard as he could go, taking rocks and little landslides with him. Behind him came gunfire, and bullets whanged off boulders nearby.

He reached the bottom of the slope and dove headfirst into brush, taking Shipwright with him. Nettles stung, but he paid no attention. Rolling over, he sat up and tried to see through the brush toward the cave. They were yelling and running in all directions. Wildcat saw the light of the lantern.

"By . . . *Jove!*" Shipwright gasped, choking for wind.

Wildcat bent over the gun in the feeble light, checking for loads. Maybe there was one left, maybe not. He twirled the cylinder.

"It was only in the last minutes," Shipwright panted, "that I realized these men were *genuine*. Beastly surprise—"

"You done fine," Wildcat growled. He twirled the cylinder again. Six holes, and Bus was a good old boy who carried an empty under the hammer for safety. Which meant that now the damned gun was empty.

"Was too bloody surprised to react at once," Shipwright muttered. "Didn't realize our lives were really in *danger*."

"We'll jus' git back outta here," Wildcat grunted, hearing the first sounds of rocks falling above as some of the gang had gotten organized and started down. "We can stay ahead of 'em. C'mon."

Shipwright gave him a ghastly smile. "Awfully sorry about this, old chap, but I suspect that I have jolly well played out my string."

With this he went limp.

"Hey!" Wildcat grated.

The author had fainted.

Sticking his empty gun in his pants pocket, Wildcat grabbed Shipwright by the back of the collar and staggered into the brush, dragging him. It was plenty black, and he was about a hundred yards ahead of Lederer's gang, but by the shouting and commotion taking place up the slope, they were now in full pursuit.

NINE

It was pitch-black, Wildcat didn't know exactly where he was going, and Ned Shipwright felt like a ton of dead meat dragging behind him. Before he had gone a hundred yards, Wildcat knew he couldn't possibly make a run for it.

Thrashing through the high grass and brush, he moved out away from the canyon walls, trying blindly to give himself maximum room to maneuver. Behind him and still up the slope, Lederer and his men were shouting back and forth, and, from the sounds they were making, fanning out to cut a swath in pursuit of him. Wildcat couldn't see a thing. Already his legs had begun to go numb, his breathing was painful, and the arm dragging Shipwright's weight felt cold and dead.

If he could make it to the creek that meandered through the canyon, he thought, he might have a better chance of lying low, or moving out of sight. But, while he knew where the creek had been up the canyon, he had no idea where it was along here. To make matters worse, he was getting out into the middle of the canyon now, and the trees had thinned out quite a lot. The only thing that saved him was the intensifying cloudiness overhead; while the thick clouds made it hard for him to know where he was going, they also made it impossible for Lederer and his men to see what they were chasing.

The shouting and everything else behind him had stopped now. Maybe Lederer had ordered silence in order to hear the prey; more likely, the quiet was in order to avoid alerting anyone else in the area.

Wildcat stumbled over fallen branches of a dead tree, twisted an ankle in a gopher hole, and limped on, dragging Shipwright. *The writer,* he thought fleetingly, *was getting badly beaten up by the dragging. Tough.*

In the blackness he couldn't see the creek gully until he fell into it.

He was looking back over his shoulder anyway, trying to make out signs of pursuit in the dense black that was punctuated only by the slightly deeper black of the far cliff wall. He was stumbling along, and then all at once his right foot plunged down into nothing and he fell forward, going head-first and taking Shipwright behind him.

He crashed down the steep dirt slope for an instant—perhaps as much as ten feet—and then hit on his shoulders upside down, bounced, and rolled over, splashing into a rivulet of cool water and mud.

Spitting, he jumped back from the water. Feeling around he located Shipwright's inert form. Wildcat bent over the unconscious man's body and put an ear to his chest. The thump of his heart was sound and steady.

Dirt was still sifting down the steep embankment over which he had plunged. As he knelt there, one leg in the water of the tiny creek, the dirt stopped crumbling down and everything got quiet except for his own breathing and the tiny murmur of running water.

It was a real granddaddy mess. In the gully it was even darker than above. By straining his eyes, Wildcat could *faintly* make out the grass-tufted earthen lip overhead. He couldn't even see the other bank, although instinct told him the gully was quite narrow, perhaps as narrow as seven or eight feet in this spot. It was a fine temporary hiding place, assuming nobody dropped in right on top of him—*which he couldn't assume*. On balance, the gully was a trap. He had to move.

Getting a handful of Shipwright's shirtfront, he staggered a few paces toward his right, upstream. The noise of the dragging body sounded like a wagon going downhill with a wheel missing and the axle dragging. That wouldn't do, especially considering the awesome quiet up on top.

Grunting, Wildcat bent and picked Shipwright up, tossing him over his shoulder sack-fashion. This worked better, but Wildcat was too staggery in the legs to move quietly with the extra burden; every step rattled in rocks or slipped in loudly sucking mud.

Cursing under his breath, Wildcat stopped again and put Shipwright down. He stretched him out nicely on the ground as far from the water as possible, then reached up and jerked down a few handfuls of the heavy grass, scattering them over the inert form. It wasn't *much* cover, but when he stood erect and squinted, even Wildcat couldn't spot Shipwright as a human form.

Now if the dadblamed boob just wouldn't wake up!

It was a chance that had to be taken.

Reaching up for a handhold in the grass that clung to the side of the gully, Wildcat shinnied up to where he was eye-level with the ground. He put his head up with great care and looked around.

The minutes in the gully had helped his eyes adjust, and he could see a little bit now. The gully ran to his right and left, an irregular dark scar in pale gray grass. The open grass extended perhaps twenty yards on all sides, and then there were the first of the stunted blackjacks, and beyond, the bigger trees. He could make out both canyon walls, about equally distant. The sky overhead was grayish-white, and in the east was the glow of lightning.

But Wildcat couldn't catch any hint of what he really needed to see, a sign of where Lederer and his men were. Straining, he could hear nothing. The wind had begun to come up, rustling the trees constantly; it didn't help.

There were two or three things that could be done, Wildcat thought. He could stay right here, and hope Lederer's men didn't stumble onto him. He could keep moving, leaving Shipwright behind, but creating enough diversion to make sure the gang followed him and left Shipwright alone. Or he could swing back around in the general direction of the cave, trying to pick up the gang visually, with the idea of slipping through them and possibly stampeding their horses.

The third possibility had considerable allure. If Lederer heard his horses running, he would have to break off pursuit and try to round up his transportation again. This would also create confusion generally, especially if Wildcat could get the animals running in all directions. By the time Lederer could get things organized again, either Jack Jackson would be around someplace near, or daylight would intervene. Wildcat didn't think Lederer would choose to remain in the canyon in either case.

The problem with this plan, however, was leaving Shipwright. The gang might find him, or he might wake up and start a commotion. *(Hell, you couldn't blame* anybody *if they woke up and found themselves covered with dirt in a creek gully in the middle of the night; the man in that shape who didn't start yelling was crazy.)*

Still, Wildcat just didn't feel he could remain where he was. He had been to a Dallas County fair once, and had seen this machine where little metal ducks went along on a trolley and you shot at them, and other little ducks just sat there. All the dudes had been shooting hell out of the sitting ducks, but the moving ones weren't even dented.

So move! Wildcat told himself.

He clambered out of the ditch and ran, bent low, across the clearing to his right. He half-expected a rain of bullets, but he made it in spooky silence, throwing himself headfirst into heavy bushes after a sprint of twenty yards.

Lying quiet to regain his breath and directions, he listened hard again.

This time, off *beyond* his previous position someplace, he heard distant rustling of brush and breaking of dry twigs that definitely could not be traced to the freshening wind. Straining, he tried to make out the precise location of the noise, but couldn't pinpoint it. It was, however, beyond his present position, and beyond the gully.

Then, somewhat nearer and to his right, he heard a dry branch crack sharply. The sound made his nerves tingle; it was maybe fifty yards distant.

He tried to figure it out, and came up with a working theory: Lederer had seen his direction of flight, and, desperate for a quick recapture, had tried to outguess him. Lederer had sent his men on a sweep straight up the right side of the canyon.

The realization gave Wildcat a chill. If he had followed his first instinct, he *would* have moved along the cliff face, and he *would* have moved deeper into the box canyon, on the assumption that pursuers would expect him to do the opposite.

He, Wildcat thought, had figured somebody might figure this, and so he had figured on the move to the center of the canyon, but Lederer, figuring that he would figure that he would figure this out, had gone on figuring on the other—

Wildcat stopped, mentally dizzy. *Whatever* the hell the

thing came down to, Lederer and the gang were sweeping into the canyon on the right-hand side, which meant Wildcat ought to be free to swing back behind them and get to the cave area again—and the horses.

Empty gun in hand, just in case it might be useful as a club, Wildcat moved out of hiding and slid back through the brush toward the cave area. He kept low, moving a few feet and then crouching to watch and listen.

It was spooky and quiet. Underneath the larger trees, pitch-blackness made him pause even more frequently. Sweat stung his eyes and drenched his clothes, and his head roared with pain from the slugging he had taken when he was captured. He knew he might have other injuries, too, but he deliberately didn't think about them. A man could handle a lot of injury if he kept in motion and didn't think about it too much.

And haste was necessary. There was no telling how far Lederer would sweep before deciding he had guessed wrong. Or Ned Shipwright might wake up and start yodeling.

Wildcat crossed a faint path that he recognized from his trip in with Teddy. He was close to the rope corral. Going to hands and knees he crept forward with extreme care, goaded by the need to hurry; at the same time knowing a guard might have been left behind.

Pressing through the brush, he reached a place where he could see through and past some trees. He caught the sound of the horses before he saw them in the dense gloom. The wind was higher now, and the lightning was nearer. Occasionally a burst faintly lighted the canyon floor, so that Wildcat could get a glimpse of the cliff and the shelf of rock overhanging the cave entry.

He couldn't see a guard anywhere. The chances were that all of them had gone on the sweep.

He couldn't wait much longer; he had to *assume* they had all gone.

Empty gun still in hand, he got to his feet and slipped out into the clearer area. His hands brushed the rope fencing the horses, saddled and nervous from the coming storm. They would run like hell, given a good kick in the backside.

Wildcat crept along the rope to the point where it was tied to a cottonwood. He fumbled at the hard, tight knots, barking his knuckles and breaking a fingernail back, well into the quick. Sucking the throbbing finger, he worked at finishing the untying job.

At this point the cold muzzle of a revolver was pressed hard into the base of his skull from behind.

Wildcat stood like a statue. The gun barrel gouged deep into his neck, punching up under the shelf of bone at the back. For an instant panic froze him this way, and he could only wait for the slug to tear the top of his skull off.

The instant passed, and he had a dozen other thoughts at once about his stupidity, carelessness, bad luck.

A voice growled, "Drop the gun *now*."

Just then lightning—the closest burst yet—flooded its veins through the clouds overhead, lighting everything starkly for a split-second.

The gun at Wildcat's head went away.

A voice asked incredulously, "What the hell are you doing *here*?"

Wildcat turned, flooded with relief to recognize Jack Jackson. "Where did you expeck me to be? This is where the gang is at!"

Jackson peered around anxiously. "Where's Shipwright? Where did they go? I was coming in slow, and heard a couple of muffled shots and some shouting and running—"

"There's a cave right up there. They had us in there. Shipwright got a gun an' we got out, runnin'. They're all up the canyon, trying to hunt us down."

"You doubled back?"

"Yeah."

"Where's Shipwright?"

"I got him hid in the gully over yonder. He fainted."

"Fainted!"

"Look, Jack," Wildcat muttered. "Gimme some shells. This gun's empty."

"Jesus God," Jackson breathed. "A madman slipping around in the dark with a gang on his heels, and Shipwright in a gully someplace, and an empty gun." He thumbed slugs out of his shell belt.

"I'm sorry I ain't doin' too hot," Wildcat said, loading his Colt. "While you was ridin' the train, I was fallin' down mountains an' gettin' my head bashed in, an' this guy about to kill me—"

"What were you going to do?" Jackson cut in.

Blinding lightning flashed overhead, the thunderclap came instantly, at deafening volume, and rain began to roar down. It came like wild, shocking rivers, instantly soaking Wildcat to the skin. It was *cold*.

Wildcat shouted in Jackson's ear the idea about stampeding the horses.

Jackson cupped his hands and yelled back: "Great idea, but they won't even hear the horses running now!"

"An' they'll be comin' back now, too!" Wildcat shouted in reply.

Jackson frowned, his face etched in grimness as another flash of lightning sizzled overhead and the rain came down even harder. "Get over on the other side. I'll stay here. When they come back, I think they'll be high-tailing it. Storm makes it impossible to hunt you. When they get inside the ropes, we'll take them."

Wildcat reached over, took a handful of extra shells from Jackson's belt, and started around toward the far side of the rope corral. *It was as good a plan as any, assuming you weren't just going to save your own skin—and Shipwright's—and then get the hell out. Which Jackson, being a lawman, would never consider. You had to get your prisoners, etc.*

But this was so much better than the situation had been a few minutes earlier that Wildcat didn't even complain mentally for long. He got to the far side of the clearing and hunkered down in soaking brush, the rain pelting into his back. It was impossible to see much, but he could make out the pile of provisions about fifteen feet away, just inside the ropes. If Jackson was right about them coming back, they would be back shortly. And they would be right here.

Wildcat waited, the icy rain making him begin to shake.

Then, through the smashing rainfall, he suddenly saw several dim figures—men's figures—coming up toward the stack of provisions.

They were back.

They slogged along, drenched and miserable. Wildcat made out Teddy by his small stature, and thought he spotted Lederer. But they were bunched and it was hard to tell.

The odds were down to four of them to Wildcat and Jackson; a lot better than they had been when Wildcat felt very much alone. The element of surprise now working against the gang helped Wildcat's disposition, too. He felt fairly calm as he watched the four men move nearer. He waited to let Jackson open the play.

The four men went under the ropes imprisoning the horses. The one who must be Teddy split the pack horse off from the others and led it to the pile of provisions. He and another figure began piling the sacks and bedrolls on the animal's back. The other two men went to saddle horses. One of them swung up into a mounted position; the other turned his horse to mount.

Come on, Jack, Wildcat thought.

Jackson came on. His rain-dimmed figure moved swiftly toward the mounted horseman from the far side, and Wildcat saw Jackson reach up, jerk him out of the saddle, and club him with a gun barrel as he fell.

Wildcat waited for no more.

Rushing forward in the mud, he caught the two men with their backs turned. He hit the first one cleanly, but the other one—Teddy—just looked too small and helpless to hit very hard. Wildcat's blow knocked his hat off, but didn't fell him. Teddy reeled around with a gun in his hand.

Wildcat closed with him and they hit in the cold mud, tangling up. He was dimly aware that all sorts of other things were going on: the horses were in an uproar and somebody was mounted and wheeling his animal, mud was flying, a shot racketed over the sound of the storm. Then Teddy's gun blared crimson inches from Wildcat's face, and Wildcat took the gun away from him and tried to wrestle for another moment. Teddy, for his small size, was a nicely dirty little fighter. He stuck a handful of mud in Wildcat's eyes and gave him a knee, at which point Wildcat knew he just couldn't mess around any longer, and slugged him a good one. Teddy went limp.

Staggering to his feet Wildcat looked up and saw *horse*—everywhere and coming right at him with a man on top. The horse reared, leaping, and a hoof smashed into Wildcat's shoulder, spinning him backwards and into the mud again. The horse went on over the ropes. Jack Jackson, slogging forward, tossed two frantic shots after the rider, but the storm had already closed around him.

Wildcat got up again. Jackson, his face smeared with red, came over. He yelled, "We got three, anyway. Better tie them fast."

A couple of the horses had spooked and knocked most of the makeshift corral down anyway, so Wildcat borrowed Jackson's knife and quickly cut some sections of the remaining rope for tying purposes. Tossing some of the rope to Jackson, he tied Teddy's hands first, being careful to leave the little man face-up so he wouldn't suffocate in the water and mud. Then, rain pelting him hard, he went over to where Jackson was just finishing with one of the others. Wildcat glanced at the man's face. It was Bus.

Going to the third man, he immediately recognized Rick, despite all the mud on him.

It had been Lederer, then, who got away.

Sharply disappointed, Wildcat tied Rick while Jackson got a couple of the remaining horses back in some semblance of calm, tying their reins to trees. The rain had begun to slacken sharply by now and Wildcat could hear things other than the storm again.

Jackson said breathlessly, "I didn't move fast enough on the big man. He surprised me."

"He was the boss."

"Damn!"

Wildcat took a deep breath which sort of hurt. "We broke it up, anyway, Jack. An' we got ole Ned safe."

The rain continued to slack off very quickly and was now already down to steady drizzle. The mud was ankle-deep where the horses had been plunging around. Wildcat carefully dragged Rick's unconscious form out of the corral area, away from the possibility of getting stepped on.

"It's going to be tough getting all the way back to town tonight," Jackson said.

"Well, Jack, we could hole up in the cave, if you got a bottle."

"Is that all you ever think about?"

"I figgered it might be useful, Jack, because I think I got a couple ribs caved in or somepin."

Jackson turned quickly, solicitous. "How bad?"

"Bad enough I want a drink. Of course *you'd* say that was normal for me, huh?"

Jackson's teeth showed as he grinned. "You said it. I didn't."

Wildcat sighed. The excitement had begun to fade with the quick-moving storm, and his legs felt like lead. "I'll go fetch ole Ned, an' we can haul outta here."

"You want help?"

"I dragged him over there, runnin'. I figger I can drag him back."

"I'll walk back and get my horse and meet you back here in a few minutes."

Wildcat stuck his gun in his belt and started to turn away.

"Incidentally," Jackson said.

Wildcat looked back at him.

The marshal frowned, licked his lips, ran his hand through his soggy hair, and finally met Wildcat's eyes with a look bordering on disgust. "I think you did a hell of a job here," he growled.

"Yep," Wildcat grinned. "I did at that."

"I don't know the details," Jackson went on, the words seemingly dragged out of him, "but if they had you in a cave, and you got yourself and Shipwright loose, you were humping. We couldn't have brought this off without you and . . . well, dammit—thanks."

"That," Wildcat replied, "is the genu-wine beauty of he'ping you, Jack. You git so dadburned thankful, you're so gracious about it, it makes my ole heart get swoled up like a toad—"

"Get Shipwright," Jackson grumbled, and turned to slog off into the muddy dark.

Wildcat chuckled and started off in the other direction. The storm was past the canyon now and only an occasional lonely big drop splattered down through the trees. As he moved out of the tree area and into the more open grass, pushing his legs through icy wet undergrowth and stickers, Wildcat glanced off to the west and saw the clouds, well off toward the horizon. The wind was down and a zillion frogs were chirping.

Trying to ignore the dull aches in his legs and the pains shooting around elsewhere, Wildcat held to a beeline across the open grass for the spot where he had stashed the unconscious Ned Shipwright. The canyon was very quiet now except for the distant roll of thunder and din of the frogs, and there was a gurgling rumble someplace that Wildcat couldn't place. Patting his soaked pockets, he tried to figure out a fast way to dry some of his tobacco and papers so he could possibly have a smoke on the way back home. It was going to be a long ride.

He figured, though, he could handle it. He really felt pretty good. For all he could tell that dull, rushing sound he heard might be in his ears; he had been socked on the head once and heard bells for a couple of days afterward. But he didn't hurt *too* badly, and even letting Lederer get away was not too damaging.

Shipwright, after all, was saved. And the gang was broken. Even old Jack had had to grudgingly admit it had been a neat trick, pulling it off. (Maybe there was a lot of luck involved, Wildcat thought, but *Jack* would never know it.)

Up ahead in the grass was the ragged scar of the gully. Wildcat saw that he had been angling too sharply, and turned a bit to stride on through the clinging, soaking grass. Up ahead a few yards was the spot he had marked in his memory.

The damned roaring sound was a lot louder.

Then Wildcat knew in an instant what it was.

"*Gawd*," he groaned, and ran.

Coming to a shocked halt on the lip of the gully, he stared down into it. He couldn't believe it for an instant. It was simply too enormous to comprehend all at once.

But hell, streams *did* this in Texas. He had known it. Everybody knew it. It was a fact of life.

Why, oh why, hadn't he thought sooner?

For the gully with a tiny creek in the bottom was no longer the same. It had flashflooded and was now brimful, filled to the very grassy lip; a rushing, turgid, muddy, chunk-studded, boiling insanity of a momentary rushing river, going at a wild speed, taking everything with it.

Ned Shipwright had been *down in there* someplace.

But, Wildcat realized in a daze, Ned Shipwright was not down there now.

He was nowhere to be seen.

The rampaging creek had taken him God-only-knew-where.

TEN

"Listen, mayor," Andy Copley said nervously, "if we wait much longer, the whole thing will git outta date. If we're gonna mourn, we gotta git with it!"

Mayor Fred Watts, standing in front of Copley's store with Wildcat, stamped his foot and turned red in the face. "Andy, you *won't* hang that damned stuff! That's all there is to it!"

Copley, a chubby man with round metal spectacles, held out the armload of heavy black bunting. "I bought up on this stuff near two years ago. The moths has been eating it to pieces. I got this great chance to sell it out cheap and git back my investment. Half the folks in town want to buy some. And you say I can't sell it!"

"This," Watts shouted back, "is Thursday. Wildcat here didn't bring the prisoners in until Tuesday morning. We didn't get men out to help with the search until Tuesday evening. The marshal and a dozen people are still out there looking. We don't even know for sure that Ned Shipwright is dead yet. I won't have Redrock going into mourning for him until we're sure!"

"How sure do you have to *be*?" Copley shot back, his eyes bulging.

"Till we find him, or find his body!"

"His body's probably down in the Gulf by now!"

The mayor turned to Wildcat. "Tell him!"

Wildcat licked his lips and said, without much conviction, "It's a fair-sized canyon, Andy. Jack still thinks ole Ned might of been washed downstream an' woke up an' crawled out someplace. They still ain't checked it all good yet."

"Then why ain't you out there lookin' yourself, Wildcat?"

"Because Jack tole me to stay here an' watch the jail an' all, that's why."

Copley held out his armload of moth-eaten black bunting. "This material," he said, "is good material. People want it. Ned Shipwright is dead and you know it. By now there's probably already a story in the papers, in places like Kansas City, how Ned Shipwright is dead. One of those writers from one of those places will come in here anytime now to do a story on it, and he'll walk down the street and he won't see any of this black material out or anything, and he'll say, 'What kind of a town is this here Redrock, that they don't even mourn a man like Ned Shipwright?' And he'll write that kind of a story back to Kansas City or wherever. I'm telling you, mayor, you got a civic duty to let me sell this material right now before the moths finish it off!"

Mayor Watts stabbed a chunky finger into Copley's vest. "You sell a scrap of that material, Andy, and I'll have you arrested." He turned and motioned to Wildcat. "Come on."

Copley called after them, "It ain't fair! I got a right to sell this good material! It's a free country! I'm an American and I got rights!"

Mayor Watts, his face brick-colored, kept walking. "Crazy, all of them," he muttered. "A man is missing two days and they get hysterical."

"Well," Wildcat said thoughtfully, "they're shocked. Hell. Ain't you?"

"No, I'm not," Watts snapped, "because Shipwright isn't dead."

Wildcat took a deep breath of genuine remorse. "I wish I thought you was right, mayor."

"You're as bad as the rest of them!" The mayor turned and stomped off in the general direction of the Silver Dollar.

Wildcat watched him go for a moment, then turned, shrugged, and walked back toward the jail with a sense of enormous sadness.

After the horrible discovery that the flash flood had taken Shipwright downstream somewhere, he and Jackson had made a frantic, futile search of the immediate area. But then a second little storm system had started moving their way, following the route of the first, and Jackson had made some decisions.

"I'll camp in their cave," he had told Wildcat, "and start looking as soon as I get some daylight. Take the prisoners back. Lock them up. Contact the mayor and Heck Sullivan. They'll know what to do. I want a dozen men out here as soon after daybreak as you can get them here. You stay in town. Take care of the jail. Get yourself repaired by the doc."

Wildcat had protested that he should hustle right back out to the canyon, since he was the best woodsman of all. Also, he felt a sharp sense of personal guilt; *he*, after all, had been the one who put Shipwright in the gully.

"I need a man in town I can trust," Jackson had shot back angrily. "I know you can handle anything that comes up, as long as you're sober. Stay sober. Remember this: Lederer is loose. There's a chance—just a chance, mind you—that he'll try to double back on the assumption that he can steal something valuable from Shipwright's room, or maybe even get some revenge on somebody like Miss Stork."

It had sounded farfetched at the time, and still did. But Wildcat had decided to obey orders. He had brought back Rick, Bus, and Teddy without incident, collecting Johnny where Jackson had hidden him on the way. Then he had gotten busy notifying the right people, and Jackson's helpers had been on the way toward the box canyon shortly after daybreak.

That had been Tuesday.

Tuesday night one of the men had come back for supplies. He told Wildcat the creek was going down fast, and they had checked its entire length in the canyon, but had found nothing.

"It looks bad," the man had said morosely.

Wednesday there had been no word at all.

Then this morning, a couple of hours ago, another of the men had come back, his right arm awkwardly tied up. He had fallen off a rock on the cliff and broken the arm in two or three places.

"We've scoured it," he had told a small assemblage of persons at the doctor's office, including Wildcat, the mayor, Freddie, and Millicent. "We've *scoured* it."

"You find *anything?*" Wildcat asked.

The man pursed his lips and looked at the floor with the stare of fatigue. "Nothin' except his hat."

"Where'd you find that?"

105

"After the crik had gone down almost all the way we found the hat down on the side, where it'd been under water a long time. It was all tangled up in roots an' tore up somethin' awful."

"Ooooohhh!" Millicent wailed, and leaned heavily against Wildcat.

"That's aw-right," Wildcat soothed her, lying. "It don't mean nothing."

The man said helpfully, "Jackson's gonna stay out there the rest of today. He's sending six guys on around the box, on the chance the crik carried the body through a tunnel in the rocks there an' into the swampy part on the far side."

So, unless something was uncovered fast, Jack Jackson and the search party would be getting back late tonight. Jackson was not a man to give up unless all hope had been abandoned several hours previously.

No matter how hard or painful it was to face, Wildcat thought, he had better start trying to face it.

Ned Shipwright was dead.

But it was a terribly hard thing to try to fathom.

Wildcat hadn't, of course, gotten to know the man very well, and a lot that he had seen, he hadn't liked too much. But there had been a certain gutty quality that was sort of nice, and maybe if you got to know him better, he was nicer. Millicent said so, anyway. Millicent might have all sorts of funny ideas, but she was no dummy. Even Freddie was truly stricken to think that his boss might actually be gone.

Then there were the stories, Wildcat thought. There wouldn't be any more. Because Ned Shipwright—that illusive, mysterious, exciting name that had appeared on so many covers—was *gone*.

Wildcat remembered putting Shipwright's unconscious body in the gully. Had he *really* been as tired as he had thought, and had it actually been necessary? Or had he been kind of hacked about Shipwright fainting? Was it all just an accident, or was he *responsible?*

It was bad enough thinking the guy was dead. But thinking that you were responsible for it was awful.

Wildcat found that he was still standing in the middle of the sunny street where the mayor had left him.

Shaking himself, he turned and trudged up toward the jail.

In the middle of the afternoon Wildcat was snoozing in the jail office when somebody came in. He awoke, instantly alert, and sat up to face Jed LaRance.

"What's going on?" Wildcat asked.

LaRance turned his hat in his hands and shuffled his feet. "Well, I jus' wanted to come by."

"Why?"

"We heard they haven't found the guy."

"Nope."

LaRance hesitated again, twirling his hat some more. He looked embarrassed or irritated, or both.

"C'mon, Jed," Wildcat suggested. "Spit it out."

"Well, dammit, we was havin' a few beers, an' we got to thinkin'. We had some fun with you an' that feller when he got to town, but we didn't count on his gettin' carried away in a durn river like that."

"We didn't either, Jed."

"Yeah," LaRance grunted. "But say, listen. Is it true the marshal an' his guys are comin' in tonight?"

"It's true."

"They ain't found him."

"Huh-uh."

"They're givin' up."

"You might say that."

"Well . . . look. What if me an' some of the fellers looked around a little? We know that country down there purty good. We might find somethin' the marshal wouldn't."

"Jed, if you want to, I don't see what harm it could do."

LaRance nodded solemnly. "Okay. I think we will, then."

Wildcat sat there and watched him walk out, closing the door behind him.

The ways of mankind, Wildcat thought, were passing strange. He had never figured Jed and his pals for very good types. But even these men were bothered by the sudden and unexpected tragedy that had fallen on Ned Shipwright.

Maybe, Wildcat thought, Jed LaRance and his pals would even find the body.

The body, even, would be an improvement over not knowing anything at all.

Wildcat got up and sauntered back into the cellblock. Bus, Rick, Teddy, and Johnny were in the big cell, and Don Keester and his two buddies were in the other. They all stood there at the bars, blinking through their beards, as Wildcat entered. Ned Shipwright had sure filled the jail.

"What do *you* want?" Rick asked sullenly.

"Nothin'," Wildcat grinned. "Jus' checkin'."

"They find Shipwright?"

"Nope."

"They find Lederer?"

"If they had of, Rick, he'd be right in there with you."

Bus said, "You won't catch him. He's too smart."

"Yeah," Teddy chimed in. "But he might catch *you*."

Wildcat walked out, assured everything was normal.

The old man from the telegraph office had come in the front while he was in the cell area. He had a sheet of yellow telegraph paper in his hand.

"What's goin' on?" Wildcat asked.

"Marshal's not back?"

"Nope. Tonight."

"Well." The old man started for the door. "I thought he'd want to see this. It's mighty interestin'."

"Lemme see it."

"Well . . ."

Wildcat took it from his hand.

It read:

MXFHHJK 66790XX   PDDY45889
DIRECTOR NATIONAL BANK
REDROCK TEX 6899000CFG
THIS TO AUTHORIZE IMMEDIATE PAYMENT $1,000 IN CASH TO NED SHIPWRIGHT, AUTHOR VISITING YOUR COMMUNITY. OUR DRAFT THIS AMOUNT PLUS CHECK FOR YOUR COSTS MAILED THIS DATE. YOU MAY WIRE THIS OFFICE NEW YORK FOR CONFIRMATION IF DESIRED.

                     T. HERRING, BIG WEST BOOKS INC.

"What the hell?" Wildcat said.

"It just came in," the old man said.

"Why are they sending him money *now*?"

"Dunno," the old man grunted. "Should I deliver it to the bank?"

"Yeah," Wildcat decided. "Go ahead."

He walked to the door with the clerk and locked it after they had gone out. He headed up the street toward the Hobnob House. He didn't pay any attention to the intense heat. Maybe, he thought, Millicent could shed some light on this mystery.

"I don't have any idea," Millicent frowned, reading the wire. She looked up at Wildcat. "It doesn't make any sense!"

Freddie, who had been napping, rubbed his eyes and scowled over the yellow sheet of paper. "Aye, it's mysterious," he rumbled.

"They got the message about him bein' kidnaped," Wildcat said, "an' *later* they send this thing, jus' like everything was fine."

"Aye," Freddie said. "They wouldna send ransom, but now they'll send money for some story."

"Maybe," Millicent suggested, "this wire was delayed."

"You mean sent before the other one?"

"It's possible."

"Huh-uh," Wildcat decided. "First, it says ole Ned is visiting *here*. So it had to be sent sometime since last weekend. Second, didn't the earlier telegram say Ned already owes a bunch of money for stuff he ain't written yet? How come would they mention that in a ransom deal if they was willin' to send him more advance money?"

Millicent, pale yet beautiful in her light blue dress, went to the window. She looked perplexed as she turned back to face them. "It's as if they thought he had been rescued or something!"

Wildcat nodded, equally perplexed. "Only we *know* better."

"I just don't understand it," Millicent said, and then began to cry.

"Aw," Wildcat muttered, and went quickly to take her

109

in his arms. "Don't cry, darlin'! Heck, we might find him yet!"

"No," she murmured, her voice muffled against his shirtfront, which was rapidly getting soggy. "We won't find him. He's gone, he's lost, a brave, noble man, struggling to document the American conquest of the West, martyred in the cause of research and accuracy."

Freddie scowled massively and smashed one of his fists into his palm. "Nay, lass, that won't do."

Millicent looked up at the angry tone of his voice. "What?"

Freddie shook his great head. "It won't *do*."

"I don't know what you mean."

"He came out here for facts," Freddie growled. "But we know he had this bloody false abduction planned. It was all a stunt. For publicity. He thought he could make enough excitement to get another advance. That's all it was."

"No!" Millicent cried.

"Aye," Freddie countered sadly. "I liked the man. But this was all a stunt. Now, if we've got a brain between us, we'll take this money at the bank for our back pay and use the rest to get us back to civilization."

"I couldn't possibly!"

"He owes us."

"I couldn't!"

"Maybe," Wildcat admitted, "Freddie's right."

Millicent wailed, "Not you, too! Oh, the betrayal!"

Wildcat was stumped and for an instant he didn't reply. He really, really liked Millicent. Perhaps he liked her partly *because* she was so implacably dumb. But he figured that right now he had to try to make her see the facts.

Slowly he said, "If Jack comes in tonight, honey, an' they ain't found ole Ned, then we gotta face it: *he ain't gonna be found*."

"No, I can't—"

"Lemme finish," Wildcat urged gently. "Now: if they don't find him, he's gone. An' he owes you the money. He liked you a lot. A whole lot. Right? He'd want you to have it. He'd *want* you to git your back pay an' all, bein' the great man he was."

This, to Wildcat, was a sentiment he could only characterize secretly in his mind as utter bullshit. But Millicent was impressed. Her face smoothed and she looked thoughtful.

"You might . . . be right," she said after a while.

"Sure I am," Wildcat grunted. "Now you all stay here an' take it easy. I got some work to do, but I'll be back to go to supper with you."

Millicent smiled wanly and gave him a light kiss. "You're such a dear, sweet man."

Wildcat left, not being able to endure getting categorized as such a hero, especially by a lovely girl who thought Ned Shipwright was a hero, too. If she figured old Ned was a hero, that said a lot about her criteria. Wildcat felt uncomfortable fitting them.

In the hall, however, Freddie caught up with him.

"I didna want to mention it in front of the lass," Freddie growled.

"What?" Wildcat asked.

"He'd sent a lot of wires askin' for money. They'd ignored them. It seems verra fishy, them sending this telegram."

"How come they would send it, then, an' now especially?" Wildcat asked.

"I don't know," Freddie admitted.

They stood there, both thinking about it. Wildcat tried to tick the facts off in some logical order:

Shipwright had asked for money and the publishers had said no.

Then Jackson asked for ransom money and the publishers said no.

Then, for no reason, the publisher sent money after Shipwright was lost.

Conclusion: publishers were crazy.

Only that didn't help.

He tried to review it all again.

Then, at once, it hit him.

"Grannies!" he muttered.

"Eh?" Freddie asked.

"Listen," Wildcat said, sweating. "Ole Ned is gone. *But Lederer is gone, too!*"

"What?" Freddie said blankly.

111

"I bet," Wildcat burst out, "that ole Ned ain't dead or lost attall! You know what I bet? I bet Lederer found him *some* damn way, an' he's got ole Ned hid out again, an' he made Ned send this wire, an' then Lederer is gonna claim the money some way!"

"Why would they send the money now?" Freddie objected.

"I dunno," Wildcat fumed. "Maybe ole Ned sent 'em a message sayin' he got rescued an' he's got this real hot story, somepin like that. I dunno, but I bet I'm *right*."

"What do we do?" Freddie asked.

"You don't do nothing yet. You don't tell Millicent or anybody else. But I got some things to do real fast."

"The poor girl would be relieved—" Freddie objected.

"Tell nobody," Wildcat insisted. "Maybe I'm all wrong. Jus' stand fast an' I'll let you know if somepin happens."

"What do you plan to do, then?"

"Go give this to the bank," Wildcat said, "an' then watch for somebody to come try to claim it. Unless I'm all wet, that person's gonna be Lederer his own self."

Freddie's barrel chest heaved in a sigh. "Aye, I hope you're right!"

Wildcat whanged Freddie on the shoulder for luck and hurried down the stairs. *This* time, he thought exultantly, he had it figured right.

It took only a few minutes to get to the bank, explain the minimum details of his theory to the banker, and win assurance of both secrecy and willingness to go along with the plan. The banker, whose name was Haverferd, was extremely distressed about what the bad publicity of Shipwright's abduction and death would do to Redrock's economy and therefore to his own business. He practically fell over backwards assuring Wildcat that things would be done as Wildcat suggested.

Then, excited about his prospects, Wildcat went back to the jail, checked the prisoners, made a smoke, and sat down to wait for notification that a man was asking for payment of the money due Shipwright.

He waited.

And waited.

Just at dark, Jack Jackson and his band of grubby, half-starved men got back to town. An impromptu delegation gathered in the middle of the street out in front of the jail. The mayor was there, Ned Bent from the Big Dollar Saloon, a lot of lesser dignitaries, and idly curious people.

"Nothing," one of the men said huskily as Jackson tumbled off his horse, staggering with fatigue.

"Nothing *at all*?" the mayor asked.

Jackson limped toward the jail, nodding curtly to Wildcat.

"Nothing?" the mayor bleated again.

Jackson turned to the mayor with the air of a man who has had it. "We've gone over every inch of that canyon. We raked in the mudholes. We climbed the side walls. We explored caves. We went without food or coffee and then we even ran out of tobacco, and it rained more, and we stayed with it, and now every one of us is worn out, soaked, muddy, filthy, frazzled, and gut-shot with hunger. And we found nothing. We're finished. Whipped. He's gone."

"Dead?" the mayor choked.

"He has to be dead," Jackson grated.

A collective murmur and groan went around the crowd, which had gotten big enough to spread all the way across the street in the twilight.

"I don't know where the flood took the body," Jackson added. "But he's got to be dead."

There was silence.

A voice in the crowd yelped, "Redrock has got to mourn! I've got black bunting on sale at my store as of now, and I say every God-fearing man in this town has a civic duty to drape some!"

The crowd, given something concrete to do, roared approval and began to break up, many men heading for the store. The mayor hung his head. Jackson limped into the jail.

Following him, Wildcat found him already stripping off his mudcaked clothing. The marshal's body looked emaciated and very white in the lantern-light, and he was, Wildcat noted idly, covered with bumps and bluish bruises.

"Jack," Wildcat said, "I got some big news."

Jackson glared at him. "You're leaving the country."

"Heck no!"

"Then it's got to be bad news and I don't want to hear it."

"Listen, Jack. I don't think ole Ned is dead."

Jackson, in the act of reaching into the wall closet for a fresh pair of pants, stopped, looked at the ceiling, and closed his eyes in pain. "God," he breathed.

"Listen!" Wildcat pleaded.

Jackson steeled himself and started dressing. "Go ahead." He sounded like he would be hard to convince.

Wildcat explained about the telegram, about the paradox it posed, about his theory on Lederer, and everything. As he told it he lost the afternoon's discouragement and believed the theory all over again.

When he finished Jackson was sitting at his desk, smoking and looking at him with very hard eyes. Jackson said nothing.

"Well?" Wildcat prodded.

"It's crazy. Impossible."

"The heck it is, Jack! It's the only dadblame thing that'll explain this whole deal! That's why you didn't find ole Ned's body, because Lederer found him!"

"Tell me this," Jackson said icily. "How does Lederer—or anyone else—figure on coming into this town and collecting that money for Shipwright when everybody in this part of Texas knows Shipwright is dead?"

The question was stunning. Wildcat hadn't thought of it.

There wasn't any answer.

"I dunno," he admitted sinkingly. "But—"

"But nothing," Jackson cut in inexorably. "The telegram had to be some kind of mistake. The thing is over. Shipwright is gone. Dead. It's closed. I'm sorry, but that's it. If you're as smart as I think you are, you'll face it."

"Aw, Jack—"

"Face it!" Jackson's voice whiplashed with fatigue and anger. Then, quickly, the marshal came over and put his hand on Wildcat's shoulder. "Look," he added softly. "I *know* you feel bad. We all do."

"It was such a durn good idea," Wildcat muttered.

Jackson nodded wearily. "I'm going to have some food. Then I'm going to turn in. Got to. I'm frazzled. Stick around till I can get a few hours, okay?"

Swallowing with effort, Wildcat nodded agreement.

Jackson limped out.

Numb, Wildcat sat around the jail for a while. The sounds of tack hammers *pinged* in the night outside. Merchants were nailing up Andy Copley's black bunting, moths and all. By daylight the town would look like one huge outdoor coffin. Wildcat got more depressed. He sent a message to the Hobnob House saying he couldn't make it for supper. Then he went over to the Mexican joint and bought a batch of beans and bread for the prisoners. They gave him a bad time.

Jackson came back and instantly fell into deep sleep on the cot.

Wildcat smoked and fidgeted, trying to convince himself that the deal was over and hopeless. But he had never accepted any deal in his whole life as completely hopeless. Something kept itching in the back of his brain, where he couldn't scratch it. He couldn't accept the situation. He didn't know why.

It must have been about midnight when he fell asleep, sitting in Jack Jackson's chair.

It was about an hour later that someone entered the office, waking him with a start.

Haverferd, the banker, stood there with a coat only partly masking his nightshirt and slippers.

"You said you wanted to know," Haverferd said, his tongue thickened by sleep.

"Huh?" Wildcat said, rubbing his eyes.

"There's a man at my house right now," the banker said, "who says he wants to claim the payment for Ned Shipwright."

ELEVEN

Wildcat was halfway back to Haverferd's house with the banker before he remembered that Jack Jackson had been asleep on the cot through it all. At this point Wildcat was much too excited to turn back for incidentals.

"Who is the guy?" he asked the banker. "Big? Tough?"

"No," Haverferd panted, hard-pressed to keep up with Wildcat's loping stride. "His name is Edwards and I know him. He works in the bank at Beauty."

"What the hell does *he* have to do with ole Ned?" Wildcat demanded.

"He says a man presented himself there for payment late this afternoon. If we'll transfer the funds to him, then he'll make payment to the man waiting to collect in Beauty."

It made sense, boy. It removed Jack Jackson's objection—a little bit, anyway. Lederer was being smart, collecting in another town, hoping it would be a routine bank transfer, and nobody would figure names too closely.

Well . . . that was still some leaky. But it was good enough, Wildcat told himself.

He led Haverferd back into his own house.

Edwards, a wizened little man who looked about two hundred years old, was dozing on the red velvet couch in the ornate living room. He was startled when Wildcat shook him, but quickly got hold of himself.

"Yes indeed," Edwards squeaked. "Yes, yes, indeed. A gentleman presented himself late this afternoon. He said he represented Nedwin Shipwright, who has a bank draft awaiting him in Redrock. Of course I was aware that a search was being conducted for the author; oh, yes, of course I was. But the gentleman presented a letter, purportedly signed by Mister Shipwright, and it occurred to me that he might have been found unbeknownst to me, and inasmuch as a rather large sum is involved—"

"Big guy?" Wildcat cut in. "Tough?"

"Well . . . yes indeed . . . rather, I should say. He had been drinking—"

"When's he s'posed to come back to git the money?"

"He gave instructions that it should be delivered to room six at the Restful Hotel."

"Aw-right," Wildcat snapped. "That's enough." He whirled on Haverferd. "Listen. Git to the jail, wake Jack, tell 'im I'm on the way to Beauty, an' to high-tail after us. Tell him the deal. You got a saddle horse, ain't you?"

"Yes—" Haverferd said, startled. "But—"

Edwards protested, "I'm extremely tired from the journey over—"

"Then sleep," Wildcat grunted. "I got the dope I need." He turned to the banker. "Show me that horse an' git goin' to tell Jack."

"But shouldn't you wait? I mean—"

There were two thoughts in Wildcat's mind. One was the urgency of the situation—the fact that he mustn't waste a moment because Shipwright's life was in danger. The second thought was more complicated; it had to do with U.S. marshals who wouldn't listen to a smart idea when they heard it, and gave up too easy. It also went to a picture Wildcat suddenly had in his mind again, a cover of a magazine or dime novel, a Ned Shipwright story, and a picture of *him*—Wildcat O'Shea—on the cover rescuing ole Ned.

"We got no time to wait for anything," Wildcat said. "We got to git movin' on this thing, fast."

Haverferd frowned nervously, but allowed himself to be pushed out his own front door to show Wildcat where the barn was located.

In four minutes flat Wildcat was up on the back of the banker's big, slightly fat gelding, crashing into the night on the road to Beauty. The horse, unaccustomed to such stern control or to being run hard, was pounding along in sheer panic, and things blurred by with crazy speed. Wildcat clung like a burr, urging the animal faster. He couldn't get there fast enough, boy. The great rescue was at hand.

It might be a good title.

Beauty in the dawn light was a sight to behold: a few dozen falling-down shacks and a couple of big 'dobe structures stuck up on the top of a bluff that looked like it might collapse at any moment. Thundering up the hill road on the faltering, well-lathered gelding, Wildcat had his plan all in his mind, and knew he was going to carry it out at once.

The time was awfully early, dawn was still pearly pink in the east, and the town was dead asleep. Wildcat rode in as far as the first buildings and sawed the horse to a dusty halt. Tying the animal at the nearest rack, he paused, legs shaking, in the doorway of a closed store to check the loads in his revolver.

The twisted street was bare, no wind stirred the yellow dust, and the rows of shacks and adobes gleamed pale in the faint light. Somewhere off in the distance a coyote yelped once and gave it up. Still shaky and out of breath, Wildcat mopped his dusty, sweaty face with his red bandanna and looked up the street, getting the Restful Hotel in focus. It was a squat frame building, one story, with a red front porch. The red on the front porch signified that all the things that went on inside were not necessarily restful, although they might be classified as relaxing. Wildcat, knowing this from personal experience, also knew that room six was in the back of the building. Therefore he walked boldly toward the structure, going right up the middle of the street.

He reached it in the same utter silence that had attended his arrival in town.

Front-step boards creaked under his boots as he went up onto the porch. Looking around, he saw no one. Listening, he heard nothing inside. He tested the screen door. It opened under his touch. He stepped into the small lobby.

It was still very dark on this, the west side of the building. But Wildcat could make out the registration desk, abandoned; the couple of overstuffed chairs and potted plants, and the black space that was the hallway which led back to the rooms.

Crossing the lobby area, he reached the corridor. The faint sound of snoring came from the nearest closed door, which was numbered 2. Wildcat crept to the next door, ascertaining that it was numbered 3, and the one across from it, 4. He peered into the gloom ahead and made out that room six was the one at the end of the hall, the one facing east; the biggest one, as he remembered it.

Spooky silence hung over the building as he moved slowly along the wall, inching his gun from its leather now and making sure that all the chambers were in working order.

He reached the door with the 6 on it. Pressing his ear to the wood, he listened.

The only sound inside—or was it imagination?—was a very faint *rubbing sound*, a little like wood on cloth or something on paper. But Wildcat couldn't even be sure it was inside the room beyond this door. He heard no snoring, no talk, no movement.

He paused for an instant, assessing the situation.

Ned Shipwright, he thought, was a prisoner on the other side. Lederer would be armed. If Lederer were awake, or had a gun close at hand, it was going to get very violent very fast.

But there wasn't anything to do but *move*.

Wildcat stepped back from the door. He was conscious of sweat soaking his entire body, the continued shaking of his legs from the crazy ride, the high intensity of awareness in every nerve ending. It was just possible that death was just on the other side of this door. But he didn't allow himself to dwell on this.

Taking a deep breath, he kicked the door down.

Wood shattered and splinters flew. The door went off its hinges, collapsing inward and taking a shower of plaster along with it. Wildcat was going into the room, gun at ready, before the door had time to fall flat.

The bed was empty.

The chair was empty.

The closet stood empty.

At a small table in front of the east window was another chair, and this one was occupied by Ned Shipwright. He had turned at the deafening entry. Wildcat, seeing everything at once, saw the stacks of manuscript pages on the table and the pen in Shipwright's hand.

"How dare you," Shipwright snapped, "burst in here in this manner, interrupting my creative period?"

"Where's Lederer?" Wildcat barked, jerking a door off the wall cabinet.

"I have no idea what you are referring to!" Shipwright retorted.

"Lederer! Lederer! The guy that's got you prisoner again!" Wildcat ran to the bed and flipped up the covers so he could peer under it.

"Stop that!" Shipwright snapped, coming out of his chair. "This is an atrocious and unpardonable act!"

Wildcat stopped, looking all around.

Shipwright was here by himself.

By himself?

"I figgered he caught you again," Wildcat said thickly. "We couldn't find you—"

Ned Shipwright, rumpled but perfectly healthy and perhaps even a little fatter around the middle in his obviously new suit, tossed down his quill on the table and stamped his foot angrily. "Is there *no* privacy or decency in this beastly country? Get out of this room this instant! If you persist in disturbing me at this time when I am at work on my manuscript, I shall thrash you personally!"

It began to dawn on Wildcat then.

Ned Shipwright had not been re-kidnaped at all. Not by Lederer. Not by anyone. He had walked out of that box canyon, and had wound up here in Beauty by accident—and the man who had asked for funds at the bank was legitimate, somebody Shipwright had hired.

And the payment in the bank at Redrock was legitimate, too, because Shipwright had let his publisher know he was okay.

While everybody else died worrying about him.

At this point Wildcat began to swear. Ned Shipwright's eyes bulged with wonderment as the words began to come out of Wildcat's chest, all the swear words he had ever heard, had ever imagined, had ever refused to think about, and then a lot more that he seemed suddenly very capable of making up as he went along. He started out by telling Shipwright how stupid he was, and then how ungrateful, and then how lucky, and then came the part about his parentage, and then Wildcat paused long enough to go over and drive a fist right through the lath and plaster wall into the room next door, and then he started all over again, and he was just getting warmed up when Jack

Jackson rushed in, gun in hand, to get his share of the bad news.

"Hold me back," Wildcat begged Jackson after explaining the situation.

"Why?" Jackson asked angrily.

"Because if you don't, I'm going to throw his ass right out the window."

"I say!" Shipwright protested.

Jackson sat on the bed, his face a mask. "You figure on opening the window first, or throwing him through it closed?"

Wildcat was so mad he couldn't even do it. He just put another hole in the wall with his fist, instead.

TWELVE

After calming down a bit Jack Jackson suggested that Shipwright explain how in the blankety-blank hell he had escaped the flash flood and then ended up way over here in the town of Beauty. Shipwright sniffed and said he would talk with them, inasmuch as his day's writing had already been interrupted by their bloody intrusion.

The first thing Shipwright had known, after fainting at Wildcat's feet during the chase, was *water* lapping around his feet. Coming to consciousness with a start, Shipwright had found himself in the gully with muddy, rushing creek water mounting by the moment and threatening to tear him downstream.

Not understanding where he was, or why, Shipwright had clambered furiously out of the gully, losing his hat in the process. Once on the lip of the gully he was bewildered and lost, and the storm was at its peak. Shipwright assumed Wildcat had been done in, so he started hiking along the creek toward the box end of the canyon.

By the time he reached the far end, soaked and shivering, he realized that he had probably made a mistake in choosing his directions. He heard sounds of men thrashing around in the rain, and barely escaped recapture by lying face-down in the muddy brush as someone walked within a few paces of him.

In a little while, however, the storm began to slack off. Cautiously checking, Shipwright determined that his pursuers were mysteriously gone. Not wishing to go back into the canyon where he might run into them again, he searched along the face of the cliff, found a rent he thought he could climb—and simply climbed out.

"Once on the far side," Shipwright concluded, "I knew I jolly well must find shelter. I soon came upon a road and followed it. It brought me to this town. When those blighters captured me they didn't even bother to search my person, so I still had a few dollars in my possession. I rented this cubicle, purchased minimum new clothing and writing supplies, wired my publishers to tell them of my adventure and the need for an advance payment, and set about creating my story." With these last words he gestured toward the tall stack of completed pages of manuscript on the window table.

"My cow," Wildcat groaned. "Why didn't you let *us* know you were aw-right?"

Shipwright reached up to adjust the monocle that was no longer there, and showed his small teeth in a grimace. "It struck me, my good man, that anonymity might be beneficial at this moment. I certainly did not wish to draw the attentions of other rapacious gangs in the area, and, in addition, the idea of having a few days of solitude in which to compose my epic was vastly appealing."

"What I don't get," Wildcat pressed, "is how these people here in Beauty didn't let us know, either."

"Simplicity itself, my good man. I introduced myself here under one of my many pseudonyms, James Nedwin. I told the innkeeper that I am an itinerant preacher. I find that Western folk tend to give the itinerant preacher a rather wide berth."

"But why did you haf to hide? I mean, couldn't you jus' as well of come on back to Redrock?"

"The adulation of the people," Shipwright sighed, "has a debilitating effect upon my muse. I realized that the adulation of your good folk would be doubled or even trebled following my adventure. Therefore, if I were to compose my novel quickly, I should remain anonymous; in exile, as it were."

Jack Jackson's teeth gritted audibly. "So you sat over here on your duff all this time?"

Shipwright eyed him haughtily. "I sense continued antagonism."

"Do you know," Jackson demanded, "that we've had search parties out? Do you know a dozen men have been combing that canyon for you in all sorts of mud and slop and storms, and one man fell and broke some bones? Do you know your lady secretary and your bodyguard are practically out of their minds with grief and worry? Do you know the whole damned town of Redrock is in official mourning?"

Shipwright beamed and strutted to the window, patting

his round little belly. "The dear people. By Jove, it is good to be loved!"

"I think," Wildcat said, "I'm gonna throw him out the window after all."

"No," Jackson grated. "It's too late for that."

"What do you suggest, Jack?"

"Get him back to Redrock. Pronto."

"Oh," Shipwright complained, turning to face them. "But I wish to remain here until the last chapters have been completed."

"You're going back," Jackson snapped. "And by God you're going back with us *right now*."

Shipwright studied Jackson's expression for a moment, and then showed his intelligence by shrugging and refusing to argue. Wildcat had seldom seen Jackson any madder, and inwardly shuddered to think what might happen if anybody argued at this precise moment.

"Very well," Shipwright sighed. "I suppose I can conclude the novel in solitude in Redrock. It will require only another day or two of creative labor."

Jackson turned to Wildcat. "The owner of this place was pretty upset when he came up to see what all our noise was about. You'd better go find him. Make sure he understands he'll get paid for the damages."

Wildcat nodded and started for the shattered door. He had to admit that he and Jackson hadn't given the hotel owner or the other guests much satisfaction when they crowded around the broken doorway a few minutes ago, demanding what was going on. He and Jackson had been so livid that their shouted explanations had been sort of incoherent.

"While he's doing that," Jackson told Shipwright, "you pack up. We're leaving in ten minutes."

"Oh, I say! I can't possibly be ready to depart in ten—"

"Now you've got *nine* minutes."

Grinning, Wildcat went into the hall.

"Wildcat?" Jackson called after him.

Wildcat turned.

"See about renting fresh horses," Jackson ordered.

Wildcat nodded and went on down the hall.

The hotel owner was shaken up, but Wildcat got him calmed down with his assurance that everything would be paid for. When the man wanted to know who Shipwright was, Wildcat made up a whopper about a wife-beater who had abandoned a bunch of kids. The man seemed satisfied, especially after Wildcat made up some gory details.

This taken care of, Wildcat hoofed it to the livery, leading his and Jackson's tired mounts. After a little haggling he rented three fresh horses, got the saddles and guns transferred, rented a rig for Shipwright, and led the animals back to the hotel.

Jackson had Shipwright on the porch, waiting.

"Let's go," the marshal said grimly.

Shipwright came down off the porch and looked up, wide-eyed, at his horse.

Wildcat handed him the reins.

"Oh, I say," Shipwright said.

Jackson, already in the saddle, looked down irritably. "*Now* what?"

"I am not—ah, that is to say—" Shipwright backed off from the horse.

"Mount up and let's go!" Jackson ordered sharply.

"Yes, of course," Shipwright stammered. "But by Jove, old man, how does one, ah, *approach* this beast?"

Jackson's eyes glazed.

"You mean," Wildcat gasped, "you don't—you can't—you—"

"Milton," Shipwright said sharply, "wrote about God and the Devil, but he was not intimately familiar with them."

It was almost too much. Wildcat felt close to tears. But he had already taken so much that a little more didn't matter.

"C'mere," he grunted. "Now. This is a stirrup. You put your foot in it an' climb up. No—*no*, goddamit! Your *left* foot."

"In the Sahara," Shipwright grunted, sweating as he tried to get his foot high enough, "the camels lie down to be mounted."

"Gawd," Wildcat breathed.

They rode out, keeping to an easy gait because Shipwright was all over the saddle like a greased rubber ball. His horse, a stout bay, sensed Shipwright's complete lack of horsemanship and kept trying to take his head and veer off the road. After a few miles of this Wildcat lost his temper, pulled a halt, got out of his saddle, walked around, and hit the horse flush in the mouth with his fist. The bay got the message, along with watery eyes, and started behaving himself.

The road was busy. They met a wagon driven by a farmer and then a little later, behind them a mile or so, Wildcat spotted the dust of a lone rider coming along after them. It was a beautiful day, not as hot as it had been before the storms, but Wildcat was not much enjoying the ride.

"If we jus' ride in an' tell the truth, Jack," he said after a while, "the town is gonna lynch ole Ned."

"I really rather doubt—" Shipwright began.

"What we'll say," Jackson cut in, ignoring Shipwright, "is that he escaped but Lederer recaptured him. We got wind of it and rode over here and jumped Lederer. There was a fight, but he got away. So now we have Shipwright back, after a bad ordeal, safe and sound."

"I really—" Shipwright began.

"Yeah," Wildcat said. "That might work. Of course we gotta git the banker in on the deal."

"I'll take care of that."

"I really rather—"

"Okay, Jack. I guess that's as good a deal as any."

"Now see here!" Shipwright snapped. "I will *not* allow this!"

"Won't allow what?" Jackson asked.

"This—this shoddy invention!"

"Buddy," Wildcat said softly, "you know what the choice is?"

"To tell the truth—"

"You jus' don't *git* it," Wildcat said. "People got *hurt* tryin' to find you. The town is covered with black material, over all the doorways an' everything else, even over Ruby's Place. If we jus' ride in there an' tell the truth, they'll tar an' feather you!"

"I simply cannot accept your theory," Shipwright snorted.

The road had led them down through some hills and now they were riding along in a small valley between several humpy rises. The area was called Mush Springs because the springs that bubbled here turned the ground into sink holes. Near the road on the right were several of these holes, one of them almost thirty yards across. Several cows had walked around the holes this morning, with the result that the grass for many feet around the water had been turned to oozy red mud. It was cool down here but Wildcat's temper was making him hotter than ever.

"Ned," he said calmly, "you better do what we tell you."

Jackson added savagely, "If you don't, we'll tell your publisher the whole thing was rigged."

"By Jove, you wouldn't!"

"Wouldn't we?" Jackson leered.

"But it was a bona fide kidnap case! You yourself—"

"We," Jackson cut in, "don't want to try to hold down a whole town of raving maniacs, and that's exactly what we'll have in Redrock if we go back there and tell the truth; that you simply walked out of that canyon and holed up in Beauty to write a goddamned novel."

"Yes, I see, but to tell my publisher, that would jolly well—"

"Then do what you're told!" Jackson snapped.

Shipwright frowned furiously. They rode along a few minutes, getting almost to the point where the road was nearest the shallow incline leading down to the bog holes and mud.

"Well?" Jackson snapped finally.

"All right," Shipwright muttered. Then his eyes flashed. "But I fail to see how such a story could be believed, when after all, here I am hale and hearty, with fresh clothing, etc."

Jackson glanced at Wildcat. "Hadn't thought of that."

"I had," Wildcat grinned.

"And?"

Wildcat reined up.

Jackson followed suit, reaching over to grab Shipwright's reins. "What do you have in mind?"

Shipwright's horse, still skittish from poor handling, tried to rear up. Jackson had to struggle for a moment before Wildcat could reply.

"Let's all git down," Wildcat suggested.

"Now see here," Shipwright protested. "It was difficult enough getting *up* here, but—"

"Giddown!"

Clumsily Shipwright complied.

"Now," Wildcat said, tying reins to a bush, "we got us a nice, clean, fresh-lookin' writer. Only he's s'posed to be beat-up an' dirty. Right?"

"Right," Jackson frowned.

"And," Wildcat grinned, "we got us here a big goddam mudhole."

Jackson's grin began to spread.

"I say—" Shipwright began.

Jackson caught one of his arms, Wildcat the other. They propelled him down the grassy embankment toward the mudhole.

"No!" Shipwright screamed. "Never! This is *beastly*! By Jove—"

Half-running with the writer between them, Wildcat and Jackson splattered into the oozy, cow-churned mud surrounding the water. Wildcat's feet began to slip out from under him and he had to let go, but he released Shipwright's arm in a kind of tossing motion. At the same time Jackson dug in his heels and heaved. Shipwright made a sound that was a little like *"Arwgh!"* and flew through the air about six or eight feet and then came down, face-first, splattering red mud and water for a mile.

Jackson looked at this spectacle, and then at Wildcat, and began laughing. He laughed so hard he fell to his knees, his hands going into the mud. Wildcat squatted in the ooze, tears falling down his face. Shipwright, spluttering and grunting, fought his way to his feet, started to rush them, fell down—his feet went higher than his head had been—and lit flat on his back.

"I suppose," Jackson gasped, holding up a handful of mud, "we ought to—be a little messy—too."

With the last word he hurled the gob of mud at Wildcat, hitting him squarely in the chest with it.

Soberly Wildcat waded out of the mud, took off his gunbelt, and laid it carefully in the dry grass. Then he added his tobacco and papers.

Another mud chunk hit him in the back of the thigh.

With a whoop he turned and charged Jack Jackson, who had also paused long enough to make sure his gun and smoking materials wouldn't get wet. Jackson was ready for him and pelted him with a big red gob, but Wildcat kept right on moving, running full-speed, and tackled Jackson around the middle, driving him backward through the goo until they hit and splashed enormously. Jackson slammed a handful into Wildcat's ear, and Wildcat got hold of Jackson's arm, swinging him around and hurling him farther out, across the whole muddy area and into the shallow, orange-colored water itself. This put Jackson very close to Shipwright, who was dazedly trying to brush himself off, and Jackson grabbed the back of his shirt and pulled him over backwards, so that he went clear out of sight under water and came up shouting hoarsely. Wildcat hurled a huge gob of mud and caught Jackson right in the forehead with it.

"By God—!" Jackson yelled, half-laughing, "everybody's wet but you!"

What the hell. After all the tension, it was really fun. So Wildcat simply charged.

He hurtled across the last of the mud and dived headfirst, making an enormous, brain-numbing belly-flopper in the water between Jackson and Shipwright. The tidal wave drenched both of them again, and Jackson instantly jumped on top of him, trying to hold his head under, and Shipwright was yelling and crying and stamping his foot in the water, and it was a hell of a mess.

Wildcat managed to get to his feet, half-knocking Jackson under again. With that splash Shipwright, who was wading out, turned sharply in alarm and fell down again himself. Laughing uproariously Wildcat grabbed Jackson's arm and fished him out. Then, spitting and spewing, they grabbed Shipwright's arms—gently, now—and started leading him up into the mud again.

"That ought to make us dirty enough—" Jackson grinned. And then he stopped very abruptly.

Wildcat, gasping yet for air, saw his friend's face suddenly change drastically.

Wildcat looked ahead, as Jackson was doing.

He tingled with shock.

Sitting on the side of the grassy bank, with a carbine leveled on them, was Lederer.

"Thanks for playing games," Lederer said. "You made it easy."

"No," Shipwright moaned. *"No."*

"What do you want?" Jackson asked huskily.

Lederer's eyes flicked to Shipwright. "Him."

"Haven't you had enough trouble? He's broke."

Lederer looked like hell. He had a week's growth of beard, his clothes were in pieces, and he was filthy and emaciated. But his grin gleamed. "Not on your life, marshal. I've been camped just outside Beauty—tracked him that far. Got a friend there. Shipwright sent off for money. I know that. I just been waiting for him to claim it before I made my move."

"He ain't got it yet," Wildcat said.

"I know," Lederer replied, eying him cooly down the barrel of the carbine. "But you came in and hurried my play. Now I'll just have to take him somewhere and figure out how to get the money from there."

Wildcat, standing beside Jackson and Shipwright in the ankle-deep mud, looked longingly toward the weapons he and Jackson had tossed on the grass a dozen paces away. Too far. Much too far. And the hammer on that carbine was cocked. Mentally Wildcat cursed himself. They should have been more alert—

"You," Lederer said, looking at Shipwright. "Come on up here."

There might have been some hope if Shipwright had stood his ground, because Lederer wouldn't want him dead. But before Wildcat could say anything, Shipwright—as if in a daze—sloshed out of the sucking mud and started up the grassy incline toward Lederer.

Beside Wildcat, Jackson murmured a single word: "Split."

Lederer didn't hear the softly spoken order, and was momentarily distracted as he climbed to his feet to stand in the roadway. Wildcat understood, however, and didn't need any more instructions.

His gunbelt lay on the grass to the left, and Jackson's to

the right, fifteen to twenty feet apart. Jackson had no intention of standing here and letting Lederer take Shipwright. When Jackson moved he would be going for one gun, and Wildcat was to dive the other way, for the other.

It would present Lederer split targets.

One of them might make it.

The other one had a fine chance of getting killed.

"Come on up here," Lederer ordered Shipwright.

The nearness of death gave Wildcat a deep chill. It was all so damned *weird:* the sun was shining, it was a great day, birds were chirping; here he and Jackson stood, covered with soaking mud and water; there was Shipwright, staggering up the grassy hill to the road like a great muddy toad; there was Lederer, a scarecrow with a gun in his hands and death in his crazy eyes. The transition from play and laughter to *this* was too quick, too shocking. Wildcat felt something as sludgy as the mud creeping through his veins. He wondered if every man felt this way once in his life—if it was a premonition of death.

Shipwright, dripping, gleaming in the sunlight with his covering of red goo, climbed up to the roadway.

Lederer reached over to the brush and jerked loose the reins of his own horse, which in their fun Wildcat and Jackson hadn't even seen or heard. Lederer, holding the carbine on them with one hand, deftly turned his horse with the other.

"Okay," he told Shipwright. "Get your horse and mount up."

"But I—" Shipwright squeaked.

"Do it!"

Shipwright went to his horse and untied the reins. Awkwardly, slipping on muddy shoes, he led the horse over near Lederer's. The horse shied a little, trampling dust, still nervous from previous mishandling.

Lederer, watching Shipwright only from the corner of his eye, repeated, "Mount up."

Shipwright threw Wildcat and Jackson the kind of look that a fisherman might get from a big trout just jerked out of the water. Shipwright was terrified, but the frown on his face showed he was struggling not only with fear, but with attempting to remember *how to get on a horse*.

Jackson said, "Lederer, the government doesn't take

THIRTEEN

The story went over 100 percent. The only trouble came when a few merchants who hadn't yet hung their newly acquired black bunting tried to return it, and Andy Copley refused to refund their money. There were a couple of fist fights over that.

Once Jack Jackson had ruled, in the absence of a judge, that Copley did not have to return anyone's money, peace returned. Ned Shipwright holed up in the Hobnob House, furiously completing his manuscript. Freddie and Millicent, once Millicent recovered from her fainting spell, hovered around the writer and ran errands for him, *shushing* everybody within a hundred-yard radius of the hotel in order to facilitate the master's work.

Wildcat, worn out and then left out in the cold by Millicent's reversion to form as Shipwright's secretary, spent two days recuperating with his regular girl, Rita.

On the following Monday he received a summons to appear at Shipwright's hotel room. Grumbling but curious, he appeared as ordered.

He found Freddie and Millicent packing and Shipwright strutting back and forth in the room, shuffling pages of his bulky, handwritten manuscript as he read it over. Shipwright had regained both his usual airs and his spare monocle, and had seldom looked dandier.

"There you are, my good man!" he said, strutting over to shake Wildcat's hand. "We have decided to depart on the afternoon train, and I wished to bid you *adieu*."

"Yeah," Wildcat said, surprised. "Thanks, Ned."

Shipwright put down the manuscript, removed his monocle, and dug into a vest pocket for several coins, ten-dollar gold pieces. "This should jolly well make some of your efforts more worthwhile."

Wildcat took the money and put it in his pocket. "I appreciate it . . . but listen, no kidding, have you gotta clear out today?"

"Of a certainty," Shipwright said. "My novel is completed—"

"You finished it?" Wildcat said with a pulse of excitement.

"Yes," Shipwright said, gesturing toward the fat manuscript. "We plan to carry it back with us as far as Kansas City and mail it from that point to New York. My publisher, of course, is in agony awaiting its safe arrival."

Wildcat eyed the package. *Boy, oh boy. Would he ever like to get into that thing and read it. He could imagine himself in it, taking old Ned around town, hunting for him after he got kidnaped, slugging people, and dragging old Ned to safety. It was going to come true, all of it. He was honest-to-God going to be a hero in Ned Shipwright's greatest story.*

"I wonder," Wildcat said aloud, "if I could jus' peek at the story . . . before you haf to go?"

"Oh, no," Shipwright replied firmly. "Out of the question. Out—Of—The—Question" He beamed and signaled to Millicent. "My dear?" He turned back to Wildcat. "I do, however, have one other memento for you. I realize that you made a strenuous attempt to be helpful, in your own way. . . ." Millicent handed him something. "Ah, thank you, my dear."

Shipwright turned back and held the package out to Wildcat: it contained four or five copies of Shipwright's books, tied together with a length of pink ribbon.

"Suitably inscribed, of course," Shipwright said, handing them over.

Wildcat, truly touched, looked at the top title. It was *Shoot-Out At Bloody Basin,* which he had already read. But opening the cover he saw Shipwright's gigantic, flowing signature, and over the autograph, in much smaller letters, the words:

To my associate, Wildcat O'Shay, from—

The name was spelled wrong, but it didn't matter. Not *too* much.

"Thanks," Wildcat said, meaning it.

"Nothing," Shipwright said airily.

Wildcat regained his composure and glanced at Freddie and Millicent, who were smilingly watching the little ceremony. "I guess I'll see you all at the depot—"

Shipwright clapped a hand on his shoulder. "My boy, take this bit of advice from a man of letters. This is a raw land, a mighty one, a savage one. Be true to thine own self. Shun the gambling hells and debauchery of painted women. Avoid the evils of rum. Live a true life, a life of cleanliness, virtue, humility, and honor. You may wish to study my works, for in these pages I have put my philosophy and my wisdom. Through the sometimes savage exterior of these epics you can find, glowing like veritable gems, the great truths and enduring values of our civilization. Guard these books well, and live life truly!"

Baffled, not knowing whether to laugh at the content or stand in awe of the style of the speech, Wildcat nodded. "Thank you."

"Jolly good show," Shipwright smiled, and shoved him to the door.

Once outside with the books clutched under his arm, Wildcat began to feel letdown. He had hoped that somehow he would have some time with Millicent before she left. He hadn't even had a chance to say anything to Freddie. Now, except for a few minutes at the train station in a couple of hours, it was all over.

The visit had been a real event for the town, he thought, sauntering toward Rita's place. Here and there you could still see a chunk of the black bunting over a door or window wherever it had been so moth-eaten that it hadn't ripped down clean from the nails after Shipwright was "rescued." Now, with Shipwright and Millicent and Freddie leaving—hell!—it was going to be dull again.

Wildcat wondered how long it would be before the new book was published. He would be famous then, he thought with a pulse. If only there was some way to get a look at the thing now!

He reached Hilda's, and went upstairs. Rita was in her room, sitting before her mirror in only the most brazen and filmy of garments.

"What did he want?" she asked as Wildcat entered.

"They're leavin'," Wildcat told her. "An' he gimme these."

Rita took the books, saw the autographs, and looked up at Wildcat with new excitement in her eyes. "Oh, honey! You must be *so* proud!"

"Yeah," Wildcat sighed. "Only. . . ."

She frowned. "Only what?"

"I *sure* would like to read this one he jus' write about me."

Rita hugged him. "It won't be long before the whole world is reading it!"

Leaving the books at Rita's, Wildcat went over to the jail. It was a little quieter. Don Keester and his buddies had been given a one-year sentence, suspended, for their planned phony kidnap job. So they were out of there. Lederer was still piled up in bed at the doc's and wouldn't be coming over with the rest of the gang to await trial for another week or two. The front office was vacant; Jack Jackson was out somewhere.

Wildcat waited.

In thirty minutes, Jackson came back.

"I suppose you heard they're leaving," the marshal grunted.

"Yep," Wildcat grinned. "Ole Ned paid me off an' give me a bunch of his books, autographed by his own self, personally."

"You get a look at the one he just finished?" Jackson asked.

"Nope, but I sure would like to."

Jackson frowned. "Sometimes, you know, these writers stray a little from the actual facts."

"Aw, sure," Wildcat said. "But heck, there ain't no way I could come out except the hero, right? I mean, you an' me, Jack, I bet we're the two heroes. Me the biggest."

"Well," Jackson said, "maybe. But there's no big thing about it."

Wildcat said nothing, being intent on making a smoke.

"Right?" Jackson said.

"Huh?" Wildcat said.

"There's no big thing about his new book."

"It's purty big for me, Jack."

Jackson licked his lips, then scowled. "You plan to help see them off?"

"Well, I expeck so."

"Okay. We'll walk over at five o'clock. There isn't going to be any ceremony. The mayor and town board will be there, but that's all."

137

"That's jus' fine with me," Wildcat said.

Jackson turned away. Wildcat wondered if the marshal was sort of glum and withdrawn, or if it was imagination. *Maybe,* he thought, *Jackson too was going to be let down after all the excitement. It was sort of natural,* Wildcat thought. *Even U.S. marshals probably enjoyed a little something different, and besides that, maybe old Jack was feeling gloomy because he was going to be only the second-best hero in the new book.*

The northbound train chugged in a few minutes early, which was practically unheard-of. Some of the people who might have been at the depot to gawk and wave didn't even get there in time. The mayor, perspiring in the dense afternoon heat, made a very brief speech saying Ned Shipwright had made Redrock the foremost cultural center west of the Mississippi, and Shipwright modestly stated that historians would accord Redrock its proper place because of the visit.

While all this was going on and the engine was snorting and clanging to get moving, Wildcat got a moment off to the side with Millicent and Freddie.

"Freddie, ole bud," he grinned, pumping the ex-boxer's hand, "it's been fun, man."

"Aye," Freddie said, grinning crookedly in return. "It all turned out well, eh, mate?"

Wildcat gave him a fake jab to the chin. "Keep your guard up."

Freddie thumped him in the belly. "Aye, and you too!"

His eyes watering from the lick in the middle, Wildcat turned to Millicent. *Her* eyes were wet, but from tears.

"Aw, you darlin'," Wildcat smiled.

She came into his arms with a little cry. "I'll never forget you," she whispered, her tear-wet cheek against his.

"Aw," Wildcat said uncomfortably, petting her.

"You gave me something very beautiful," she whispered, "and you saved his life."

The engineer clanged the bell and hit the whistle a lick. Steam vented from the boiler and the wheels grated.

"Aaaaaaboooard!" the conducter yelled.

Laughing and crying at the same time, Millicent kissed

Wildcat again and ran for the passenger car. Freddie, waving, followed and Ned Shipwright shook hands all around, then strutted back to the stairs, stepped up on them, turned, and gave a little salute. The engine steamed and huffed, and began to move. The big steel wheels spun on the rails, the train began to pick up speed, and the passenger car glided past, so that Wildcat got a last glimpse of Millicent dabbing at her eyes and Freddie, a big grin splitting his ugly puss, in one of the windows. Ned Shipwright remained poised in the open doorway, grandly holding his hands aloft in benediction, with the sunlight glittering gold on his monocle.

Then the cars slid past the end of the depot and out of sight behind the warehouse next door.

The ground still shook from the engine's power and soot began falling all around on the platform.

The mayor and town board looked at one another, sighed, and trooped off. The few others who had come by to watch also began to break up and sift away.

Wildcat turned and saw Jack Jackson starting away, too.

"Wait up, Jack!" Wildcat called, and hurried to join him.

They walked around the depot and into the street. The crowd had already broken all up and off to the north, from a great distance, came the last hoot of the engine.

"I guess that's it," Wildcat said.

"I guess so," Jackson said. He was trudging along with his head down.

"Next thing we'll know, that book'll be here."

Jackson said nothing.

"Man," Wildcat said, "I can't wait."

Jackson was silent.

"Can you?" Wildcat asked.

"What?" Jackson grunted.

"Can you wait?" Wildcat asked.

"It's no big thing," Jackson snapped.

"Aw," Wildcat grinned, "I bet you're jus' put out because you're gonna be the number-two hero, instead of number-one, which *I* am. Right?"

They had neared the Hobnob corner, and Jackson

lengthened his strides. "Let's forget it," he said.

"Man, how *can* you forget it? I mean, when that book comes out—"

"What makes you think we're heroes in the stupid thing?" Jackson asked angrily, whirling to face him.

Astonished at the anger on his friend's face, Wildcat stood rooted. He didn't get it. "This is the second time today you've said the book ain't important," he remembered. "What's the matter, Jack? Are you modest or somepin?"

"Writers," Jackson said levelly, "don't follow facts."

Wildcat then had a glimmering. "Hey! *Have you read the book?*"

"No," Jackson said. But his face said the opposite.

"You have!" Wildcat cried. "Grannies! How were you in it, Jack? How was I? Did he use our real names? What do you look like? What does he have us say?"

"Forget it!" Jackson ordered.

Wildcat grabbed his arm. "No! Hey, you've *read* it! Listen, you gotta tell me! How did *you* git to read it?"

Jack Jackson's lips were white. "Shipwright brought it over. He said he needed someone to check a few of the facts."

"Like what we really said—like that?"

"Hell no!" Jackson exploded. "Like the names of hills and towns. Any other resemblance to real people is an accident!"

"What do you mean?" Wildcat demanded.

"I," Jackson grated, "have had one or two sociable drinks in the last year. I don't gamble and I don't jolly the girls. People *respect* me."

Wildcat stared at him, soaking up the rage yet unable to make it make sense.

"I don't git it, Jack," he admitted.

Jackson pointed at his own chest with his thumb. "Am I really a drunk? Do I really spend my nights in Hilda's?"

Wildcat tumbled. "You mean—in the book—you're a *drinker?*"

The look on Jackson's dark face gave the answer.

"You mean," Wildcat said, suddenly doubled up with glee, "in the book *you chase gurls?*"

Jackson started to turn away.

"HAW!" Wildcat roared. "That's the funniest thing I ever heard! Oh my gawd, that's priceless! You mean he made you in the book into a drunk an' a guy that chases the gurls? HAW! HAW!"

Jackson spun back. "Do you know what *you* are in the book?"

Wildcat stopped laughing. "Huh-uh."

"You'll find out when the book comes out," Jackson spat. "Maybe it's better for you to know now, so you can start getting used to it. With Shipwright out of town I guess it's safe enough to tell you."

Wildcat stared, not at all sure now that he wanted to know. "Don't fun me, Jack," he warned.

"You," Jackson said, "are an idiot. In the book. You're just flat-stupid. You wear these loud clothes and you fall over your own feet. You know when Shipwright got kidnapped? Do you know where he has *you* in the book right then? You're over at the church———"

"The *Babtist* church?" Wildcat shrieked.

"———mopping the floor," Jackson said icily. "Because that's the kind of work you can handle. And when the rescue comes, do you know what you do?"

"I guess I walk in, guns blazin'———"

"You faint," Jackson said.

"What?"

"In the book," Jackson went on grimly, "I'm a fool and you're a clown. The only real difference is that I'm also vicious and cowardly. You fall on your ass and throw up, and things like that. And do you know who the hero is?"

"No," Wildcat said. "I dunno, but I don't wanna———"

"*He* is."

"Who?"

"Him!"

"Shipwright? His own self?"

"He does it all," Jackson snarled. "He saves our lives. He puts everybody in jail and then he rides off on a big stud horse, the hero, with women and little children crying because he was so beautiful."

"I don't believe it," Wildcat said. He believed it.

Jackson spat, eyed him for a glowering moment, and walked away.

Wildcat stood there, stunned beyond movement or rational thought.

It was just too much. It was true—he *knew* it was true, but it was too much.

Ignoring the sound of several horsemen coming up the street, he walked slowly right up the middle, hands jammed in his pockets.

Hell, it was heartbreaking. After all the hero-worship, all the trying to help the so-and-so, that last little speech, the whole gizmo—for the no-good louse to turn right around and write a book that made you out a clown, somebody everybody would laugh at.

"O'Shea!"

It was unendurable. His confidence in human nature was shattered. His idealism was gone. His life was ruined. Life was no longer worth living. He had had it, he was finished, he was crushed and betrayed, all he wanted to do was curl up and quit.

"O'SHEA!"

This time he heard the angry voice and turned.

The horsemen had reined up alongside him, right at the alley entrance. For an instant, as they staggered out of their saddles, Wildcat didn't even recognize them. They were the rattiest, sorriest, most miserable, dirty, bedraggled bunch he had ever seen. Their clothes hung in tatters, one of them was barefoot, they were covered with mud and manure and dust, one of them had a broken arm, they smelled as bad as they looked, and they appeared half-starved on top of everything else.

Then Wildcat began to recognize faces behind the dirt and beards.

Jed LaRance. Dick Bruniston. Buster Davis. Jug Wonfor. King Wilson.

But good lord! They all looked like scarecrows.

Wildcat walked over to where they stood beside several stacked garbage cans in the mouth of the alley. "You guys look awful! What—"

"You found him," Jed LaRance said.

"Huh?"

"You found him t'other day," LaRance said, as if in a daze. "You brang him back—now he's left town."

"Oh, grannies," Wildcat said, remembering.

"We said we'd go hunt," LaRance choked. "We hunted. You never sent nobody out to tell us you'd found him already."

Dick Bruniston said, "We could of *died* out there."

"We almost did," Buster Davis croaked. "We thought we was doing a good thing—"

"But you never even *told* us he was safe," Jed LaRance said.

"Aw, fellers—" Wildcat began, spreading his hands.

Jed LaRance stepped forward and hit Wildcat flush on the mouth. The blow knocked Wildcat over backwards and by the time he got his eyes open, the whole gang of them had descended on him.

Giving somebody an elbow and someone else a knee, Wildcat hit LaRance's ear and stuck his fingers down somebody's throat, and gouged a spur to a leg, and came up kicking and swinging. He knocked Buster Davis clear over backwards and upside down, and then someone hit *him* in the back with crushing force, driving him forward off-balance.

As he crashed into the stinking garbage cans, knocking them every direction, Wildcat reflected briefly upon the nature of life. He had been disappointed in Ned Shipwright. But what the hell. He was still Wildcat, and nobody could take that away from him. What did he need a book written about him for, anyway?

His momentum carried him on through the spilled garbage cans and into the brick wall, where he sprawled for the split-second it required for King Wilson to try to kick his face in. Wildcat spun, caught Wilson's leg, and twisted. Wilson went down, accidentally falling into Jug Wonfor, who crashed face-first into the brick wall knocking out just an *incredible* number of teeth. Then Dick Bruniston was in the front again, diving at him and screaming obscenities, and out in the street a woman was screaming and people were running and a horse had bolted with a wagon, throwing drygoods all over the street, and Wildcat wound up and brought up a haymaker that connected solidly with Dick Bruniston's chin, caving him in to the side just as somebody else lit on him, biting, gouging, and taking him down again under an avalanche of muddy, stinking, enraged humanity.

This is fun! Wildcat thought, whaling away with both hands.

And life *was* worth living, after all.

Wildcat tossed the man off his chest, sledge-hammered Jed LaRance with an elbow, and swung a garbage can. But everybody was so crazy with anger, they just kept getting up and charging again. *If Jack Jackson or somebody didn't spoil it,* Wildcat thought, *this was surely going to be the greatest fight of his entire life. And, by golly, he intended to make the most of it.*